# Fall I[n]

## 202[0] Edition

With Stories from:

Jessica Chanese
S. A. McKenzie
David Powell
Bethany A. Perry
Alex Minns
Chris Bauer
Mato J. Steger
David Cleden
Jess Ko
R. A. Clarke
S. E. White
Elyssa Campbell
Amy de la Force

Published by:
Cloaked Press, LLC
PO Box 341
Suring, WI 54174
http://www.cloakedpress.com

Cover Design by:
Steger Productions Design
https://fantasyandcoffee.com/SPDesign/


ISBN - 978-1-952796-00-5 (Paperback)

# Table of Contents

The Scribnery by Jessica Chanese ........................................4

First Encounter by S. A. McKenzie.................................17

Three A.M. Challenge by David Powell ........................34

The Magnificent Hat by Bethany A. Perry....................51

The Prisoner's Cage by Alex Minns............................78

World of Your Dreams  by Chris Bauer ........................107

Stardust & Lies by Mato J. Steger................................118

Museum of Lost Souls by David Cleden ......................130

When the Last King Dies by Jess Ko ...........................153

Mr. Regret by R.A. Clarke ............................................169

The Princess in the Tower by S. E. White....................200

Slay a Fledgling by Elyssa Campbell............................209

The Overlander's Poison by Amy de la Force.............234

Thank you…............................................................245

# The Scribnery
## by Jessica Chanese

I sat in an overstuffed armchair, staring across an expanse of mahogany desktop at Malfi Rockwood, Head Scribnerian. She busied herself with scrutinizing each page of a file conspicuously marked with my name, although I knew she would have thoroughly vetted my qualifications and background before inviting me to the Scribnery for an interview.

Scribnerian posts were highly sought after. Most Charasmati would kill to be in the seat I occupied, and rumors abounded that more than a few had. Rockwood wanted to be sure I was very aware of my good fortune to find myself in her presence, with a potential Scribnery job hanging in the balance, no less.

I kept my expression neutral and my body language relaxed and open. If the Head Scribnerian wanted to see me rattled, she would be disappointed. For high-ranking Charasmati like Rockwood, there was no currency more valuable than power. To appease her in the name of achieving my ultimate goal, I'd need to balance on the knife's edge between arrogance and deference.

After several more long moments of seemingly dissecting each syllable on my resume, Rockwood pretended to have stumbled on an unexpected detail.

"So you're a Synthesi? How delightful!" the Head Scribnerian trilled through shockingly coral lips.

Her feigned surprise rang hollow. I knew my status as the last known living Synthesi in the Charasmati world was the only reason she was considering my application.

Rockwood set my file aside, turning her full attention on me. She bared white teeth in what was probably meant to be a welcoming smile, but read more like a predator's warning. Then again, maybe that was her intention.

"As a Transformagi on the higher end of the power scale, I've never envied my fellow Charasmati's talents. Why would I, when I can mirror them with my own superior gifts? But a Synthesi …" She gave her head a little shake and flashed me another a wide predatory grin. "Why, my dear, you possess one of the few gifts - well, the *only* one we know of, really - that a Transformagi *can't* mimic. The ability to see inherent connections between disparate elements and intuitively weave them into spellwork is a rare and potent magic. Your talents could be well-used strengthening the Scribnery's castings."

I gave the Head Scribnerian the gracious smile she was seeking, then waited patiently for her to continue.

"Professor Atherton gave you a, well, positively glowing recommendation," she said, with a bird-like tilt of her head. "She seems genuinely impressed by your performance during your time under her tutelage. Not only that, but her letter conveys genuine affection for you. No doubt you realize how … uncharacteristic … of her that is." She eyed me with suspicion over the absurdly blue acrylic frames of her glasses.

5

Rockwood had some interesting aesthetic preferences, which was probably the only trait of hers I would find remotely appealing.

After a five-year apprenticeship, I still couldn't articulate why Katarine Atherton and I got along so well. She was arguably the most well-known misanthrope in the magical community, not that anyone blamed her. Atherton was, by all accounts, the strongest Empath of her time. It was easy to understand why someone who was constantly bombarded by the emotions of others preferred solitude.

It was somewhat easier to explain why she agreed to take me under her wing when it had been decades since she entertained a formal mentorship. Her empathic magic paired with a particularly developed ability to perceive power signatures enabled her to sense the full breadth of my gifts - and my intentions for them - as soon as I crossed the threshold of her study. Atherton was too canny to pass up the chance to mentor the first Synthesi to come along in generations.

What almost no one else knew, though, was that Katarine Atherton desired the demise of the Scribnery as much as I did - and she knew I had the juice to make it happen.

"Professor Atherton and I have a mutual admiration for each other's talents. I don't know that she truly *likes* me anymore than she likes anyone else, but she tolerates me and respects my abilities. I'm grateful for her support," I responded.

"Splendid," Rockwood said flatly. "Well, Ms. Marin - "

"Please, call me Shoni."

Rockwood's eyes narrowed at my interruption. "Shoni, then. I'm happy to report your application for the position of Junior Scribnerian has been accepted. You'll start Monday. Welcome aboard."

***

Rockwood met me in the Scribnery's reception area, accompanied by a fresh-faced young woman who stuck out a hand and introduced herself brightly.

"Millie, the intern, pleased to meet you!"

I gave her hand a brisk shake and ventured a friendly smile. "Shoni, new Junior Scribnerian. Likewise."

Scribnery internships were hard to come by. There was a good chance Millie's family packed some serious clout in the Charasmati social hierarchy. Making allies here, especially those too green to have completely adopted the Scribnery's dogma and who probably had a slew of influential connections, could only help my cause.

"Right then. Follow me, please," Rockwood directed.

The Head Scribnerian motioned for us to come along as she strode down a long corridor, stopping in front of an imposing arched metal door. Rockwood muttered an incantation and the door swung open, revealing a cavernous multi-story space bustling with activity.

Scribnerians filled desks and cubicles on the ground level and throughout the balconies lining the room's periphery. Some stood in small groups apart from the main workspace, partaking in cooperative spellwork or engaged in discussion.

Scanning the room, I noticed a gauzy partition blanketed the space from floor to ceiling in place of a far wall - the cloaking spell separating the Scribnerian's workspace from the Scribnery itself.

When we came to a stop in front of the veiling enchantments, the Head Scribnerian began another incantation. The filmy veil disintegrated.

I had researched the Scribnery for years and seen hundreds of photographs and drawings of it in the process. I'd read countless descriptions of both its appearance and the enchantments on which it operated. Encountering it in person still took my breath away. Infinite rows of writing instruments, levitating at varying heights and moving of their own accord, stretched beyond what the physical boundaries of the room should allow.

The endless field of pencils and pens in fashions spanning the ages, including the occasional quill and stylus, was a blur of motion as they danced over everything from spiral bound notebooks to rolls of parchment and electronic tablets. Typewriters, desktop computers, and laptops were interspersed among the manual writing instruments. Each represented the unfolding Story of a life - the life of a Non-Charasmati who would never know their every decision was predetermined for them by what was essentially the magical equivalent of an algorithm-driven computer program.

Rockwood practically glowed with pride. If nothing else, it *was* an impressive feat of spellwork.

"Why are some of the writing instruments so much older than the others?" Millie asked.

"Stories are transcribed in the fashion common during the time of one's birth," the Head Scribnerian answered in a clipped tone. "You should know that much."

The intern was undeterred. "Well, yes, I knew that. But I don't understand why Stories that appear to have begun centuries ago would still be active in the Scribnery."

"A person's Story doesn't end with their death," Rockwood chided. "The Scribnery keeps all Stories active until there is no remaining trace of a person's existence on Earth. Our spellwork guides how each Story's protagonist is remembered in perpetuity."

I suppressed a shudder. Even after death, the Scribnery's magic dictated the course of a Non-Charasmati's legacy.

\*\*\*

I was sixteen-years-old when I learned about the Scribnery. It was immediately after saying goodbye to my closest childhood friend for what would be the last time. He had inexplicably enlisted a few months earlier, and was preparing for what would be both his first and last deployment.

*"You don't need to go, Piro. Please don't go," I pleaded. My eyes were red-rimmed and swollen from a sleepless night full of tears.*

*My best friend's normally twinkling eyes were distant. "Yes, I do. But it will be okay, Sho Sho, I promise."*

*He reached up to touch my face and my tears fell freely again. With a sad smile, Piro kissed the top of my head, then vanished through our front door. I fled to my bedroom and threw myself onto my bed, burying my face, and my tears, in my pillow.*

*My sister, Emmaline, rushed to comfort me, sitting on my bed and pulling me into her arms. I sobbed into her shoulder.*

*"It's just so unlike him, you know? He never once mentioned wanting a military career before he signed up." I wiped my face with the back of my hand.*

*Emmaline stiffened. I pulled away, searching her face.*

*"What is it, Emmy?"*

*"I'm not supposed to tell you, yet. But, you'll find out in just a few short years when you go to the Academy anyway. If you promise not to repeat a word of this until then - not a single word, Shoni! - I guess it wouldn't hurt to tell you now," Emmaline said with some uncertainty.*

*"You know I'll always keep your secrets -"*

*"It's not just my secret. It's much bigger than that."*

*"Okay, okay. I promise. Now, please, tell me what you're getting at?"*

*Emmaline fidgeted with the hem of her dress. "There's something you need to know about Encies," she said, using the slang term for the Non-Charasmati, or "N.Cs" - people like Piro who didn't have magic. "You've learned about what happened in the first few centuries following the Charasmati Revelation, right?"*

*I nodded. "Of course. That's basic history." Charasmati children learned early about the Revelation, when a group of Ancients became aware they possessed abilities typical humans did not. Over time, the Charasmati grew into a complex and powerful magical community, living in parallel to Non-Charasmati society without their knowledge. While the Charasmati cultivated their abilities and used them to create a prosperous and peaceful future for their people, the Non-Charasmati struggled through all manner of ills and evils. Charasmati weren't immune to the disasters that befell the Non-Charasmati, but they were better equipped to mitigate the damage. The Charasmati Ancients eventually found a way to channel their magic in order to stabilize life on Earth, for both the magical and non-magical.*

*"Right. So you know that after a few generations of chaos reigning, the Charismati Ancients were concerned about the fate of humanity. They questioned the capability of those without gifts to navigate the challenges of mortal life," Emmaline explained, as if I hadn't heard the same lecture countless times before.*

*I rolled my eyes. "Yes, Emmaline, I know all of that. Get to the point, please!"*

*My sister crinkled her nose at my impatience. "Have you ever wondered what, exactly, they did to rectify the problem?"*

*I stared at her blankly. The truth was, I hadn't really. We were taught the Ancients found a way to funnel their magic to make the world safer for all humanity.*

*I knew whatever they did wasn't a perfect solution, of course, but I'd never given much thought to the details.*

*Emmaline sucked in a breath, as if bracing herself for the fallout of whatever news she was about to deliver to her unsuspecting younger sister.*

*"They built the Scribnery," she said in a rush. Before I could ask what that meant, Emmaline forged on. "The Scribnery houses all of the Encies' Stories, the records of their lives. But, it doesn't just store them ... it* writes *them."*

*My mouth gaped as I processed what Emmaline was telling me.*

*"How?" I asked, horrified.*

*"An Encie baby's birth triggers a spell at the Scribnery. The spell manifests a writing utensil - usually a pen of some sort, but sometimes it's a pencil or some such, whatever's common at the time - that composes the Story of the Encie's life. An Encie's writing instrument doesn't define the essence of who they are. There's no magic strong enough to override the human soul," Emmaline paused, appearing to weigh her next words carefully. She could sense my rising agitation. "But, it does dictate their path. The charms and spells cast by the Scribnerians - the spell-wardens of the Scribnery - guide the Encies' life stories in a manner most in harmony with the needs of society as a whole," she concluded.*

*I jumped off the bed in a fit of anger, my fists clenched so tightly that my fingernails bit into my palms. I'd grown up thinking of the Charismati as the magnanimous chosen who used our given abilities for the greater good, only to find out we were just a shadow society of narcissistic puppeteers.*

*Emmaline stood. "We're Charismati, Shoni. We're The Gifted. It's our duty to use our powers to help those less fortunate," she said.*

*"Less fortunate? Piro is less fortunate? He's our friend, Emmy. He's nothing less than either of us, or any of the Gifted. He's always been the best of us and you know it. He did absolutely nothing to deserve having his free will taken from him!"*

*I was yelling then. Emmaline cowered, but I didn't care. I was consumed with righteous indignation toward the unimaginable hubris of my kind.*

*I knew then I would right this wrong. The Scribnery had to be toppled. I didn't know how, but I was certain I'd figure it out.*

***

Three months into my employment with the Scribnery, I'd carefully studied their security measures and staffing patterns. I had worked out when I'd have the greatest window of time to cast the spellwork that would put a permanent end to the Scribnery - and put control of the Non-Charasmati's destinies back into their own hands. This afternoon, during the monthly staff meeting, was my best shot. I was ready.

*"Remember, Shoni - a casting of this magnitude will drain you more than you've ever experienced. It has the potential to deplete your power reservoir permanently. When you finish the spell, the Scribnerians will come for you, and you will not be able to use magic to evade them,"* Atherton had warned.

The glimmer of hope in her eyes when we last spoke had belied her dour demeanor. A lifetime of absorbing others' feelings - and being privy to the jarring disconnect between the Encies' behavior and their emotions - had taken their toll. Katarine understood the injustice being inflicted by the Charasmati through the Scribnery more intimately than anyone else could fathom.

About halfway through the mandatory staff meeting, I discreetly made my exit. I hurried to a spot on the Scribnery's workfloor, just before the start of endless rows of writing tools in constant motion, and hastily arranged my supplies. I took a moment to appreciate the magnitude of what spread before me. The depth and intricacy of the Scribnery's magic, and the reality that it held the Stories of millions of human lives, was humbling. And then it was time.

*"You'll only have a few minutes to complete the casting."* Atherton's words echoed in my head. *"'Drink the potion, find the threads, say the incantation, sublimate the Stories. Got it?"*

The potion Katarine brewed would heighten the sensitivity, and broaden the scale, of my Sythesi magic to a level which would be untenable for more than a few minutes. In those brief moments, I'd be able to see the invisible threads connecting each writing implement in the Scribnery to the human whose life story it was writing. I would need to speak an ancient charm we'd unearthed that would create an alternate psychic connection between each Encie and the instrument transcribing their Story. And then, using every ounce of my power and skills, I would sublimate the writing instruments into the consciousness of every living Encie. To the best of our knowledge, the sublimation would be irreversible.

*"Drink the potion, find the threads, say the incantation, sublimate the Stories."*

And so I did.

I can't describe what it felt like - the tidal wave of magic rushing over and *through* me as I subverted the Scribnery's fastidious spellwork. The beauty of the spiderwebs of glittering threads linking each Story to its rightful owner. It was mind-bending and surreal and exhilarating.

Afterward, I lay on the cold stone floor, near delirious from the surge of power I'd just channeled. Atherton's warning bounced around in my throbbing head. I steadied my breathing and attempted a simple charm. Nothing.

Strangely, I felt only relief.

The workfloor was quickly filling with harried Scribnerians, shouting or staring speechlessly at the barren room. Alarms blared announcing the obvious security breach.

Rockwood marched to where I lay, her face drained of color. "What have you done?"

I could only smile.

***

By evening, the Encie press was awash in reports from across the globe of citizens feeling as if a fog was suddenly lifted from their awareness. How, for the first time in their lives, they felt fully present and whole.

Encie historians would refer to the day the Scribnery fell as one of an inexplicable collective awakening, presumably caused by cosmic phenomena beyond human understanding.

I read and reread the articles in the confines of the cell where I'd live out my days, content with knowing all humans would now be the authors of their Stories, as it should have always been. With each article I read, I relived the day so many destinies were handed back to their rightful owners. And each time, I could only smile.

**Jessica Chanese** is a speculative fiction writer living in Upstate NY with her husband, two forces of nature masquerading as their children, and their two dogs. She's had short stories published in Black Hare Press' Lust anthology and Verse of Silence literary magazine, and has written an as-of-yet unpublished full-length contemporary fantasy novel. Fantasy, urban/contemporary fantasy, and magical realism are her favorite genres both to read and to write. You can find her on Twitter at @jchanese or on Facebook at Jessica Chanese, Writer.

# First Encounter
## by S. A. McKenzie

My uniform shirt was sticking damply to my back. I plucked it away from me, automatically bracing myself as the creaking bus juddered across a series of potholes. My irritation grew with every bounce. What was the point of being a DROCA field agent if you had to take public transport? And not even an inner city bus, but this antiquated barely-functioning bolted-together collection of pre-apocalyptic scrap belching and groaning its way around the outer limits of Seattle.

To distract myself from my discomfort I begun to run through a telepathic drill, touching each passenger in turn with a feather-light brush of mental contact. Not prying into people's secrets, just getting a quick impression, looking for threats and anomalies like I'd been taught. The passengers were mostly agricultural workers heading to the urban farms or students on their way to school. I flicked through them, getting a series of surface impressions: <my back's still sore, hope we're not weeding today>, <but does he like me?>, <gonna flunk this test>. There was a psi at the back of the bus. He looked up briefly, gave me a faint smile and the mental equivalent of a fist bump. I found another one near the front. She kept on reading through the pile of documents on her lap, projecting an image of a closed office door <busy, can't chat>. I went through the whole bus until I got to my partner Kevin opposite me, looking annoyingly immaculate and unruffled, as elves do. As always his shields were an impenetrable wall of granite. I gave them a flick anyway and bounced off, annoyed, and moved on to the old witch

17

next to him, a little harder than necessary. She jumped like I'd goosed her, setting the black rooster in the lidded basket on her lap clucking and scrabbling, then glared at me. Oops.

I almost returned her glare with my best bad-ass stare but remembered I was in uniform and officially representing the Department for Regulation of Changeling Affairs. According to previous instructions from my supervisor, glaring at members of the public is not appropriate behavior for an agent. Instead, I gave her a small polite smile and feigned an intense interest in the passing scenery. Thankfully our stop was coming up, and we began the process of extricating ourselves from the rest of the human cargo before the bus jerked to a halt.

A multi-colored wall of shipping containers piled three high stretched out in both directions, marking the boundary of the Salvage District. The vast metal gates were open and busy with traffic in both directions: loads of unsorted material brought in by the deconstruction engineers working to dismantle the suburbs was going in, and merchants who'd purchased items for their shops and stalls in the city were coming out. We stopped to check-in with the gate guard who directed us down a side street.

"I really don't see how it benefits the city having agents waste their time on the Crank File," I groused, as I followed Kevin past giant warehouses and yards where workers sifted through the detritus of pre-Change civilization. With the trade routes mostly closed these days, every last scrap had to be saved and re-used because we weren't going to get any new raw materials any time soon.

"You know the department is legally required to investigate every possible sighting of a magical creature that could present a danger to the city."

"I know that! I just don't see why you couldn't pick out the likelier ones first." Kevin had been on the team six months longer than I had, which meant he had seniority, and I was supposed to do what he told me.

"Just look at what we've had this month." I counted them off on my fingers.

"A cockatrice on the loose in Washington Park—which turned out to be just a rooster with a lot of missing feathers. And the ghost of some dude named Elvis—big deal, there are ghosts everywhere—except he was supposedly driving a fossil-fuel powered Cadillac, and I don't know where anyone, let alone a ghost, would get the gas."

"That rooster was a public menace. It took two of us to subdue it. Anyway, what about the flying saucer and the alien abduction? That was interesting, wasn't it?"

"That so-called 'abductee' threw up on my best pair of boots! They still reek of moonshine-flavored vomit on hot days. I'm going to have to buy a decontamination spell."

"He did have some very intriguing theories, though."

I rolled my eyes. These weren't the sort of career-making cases I deserved. At 19, I was one of the youngest recruits ever to complete DROCA training. I was itching to start getting team assignments and make a name for myself. Instead I was still on probation, and now they'd paired me up with an elf, of all people. Elves had to be my least favorite type of changeling. Back when I was a kid and my Mom worked at the mayor's office, occasionally she'd take me to work when I was sick and she couldn't find someone to watch me. A delegation from one of the northern elven enclaves came in one time. They were all smiles and charm and pretty hair on the outside, but inside of them all I could pick up was cold calculating ambition. Touching their minds felt like bathing in slime. I couldn't imagine why an elf would want to become a field agent, but DROCA was an equal opportunity employer and Kevin outranked me, so I kept my mouth shut. Mostly.

"We could have at least gone to check out that centaur sighting at Ames Lake. They'd have let us have a car for that, Kevin!"

"Centaurs are anatomically unlikely," Kevin said without looking back at me. "Anyway, it's a lovely day for a unicorn hunt."

I mopped my face and glared at his back. Hardly anyone had personal vehicles these days, since fuel supplies were limited. One of the perks of being a DROCA agent was the motor pool. I'd had visions of myself speeding down the road in one of the official black SUVs that matched my uniform, but as yet I hadn't even scored a ride as a backseat passenger.

"I'll bet you ten bucks we're just going to wind up chasing some scrap dealer's lost pony, if there's anything there at all. I mean, how on earth would anything on four legs get past the district walls without being seen?"

Kevin just shrugged in an annoyingly elegant manner, and I gave up trying to reason with him. Four dusty hot blocks later and we found Jim's Salvage, surrounded by a rusty chain-link fence. The lot had been one of those places that rented storage units before the Change. The sign on the gate read 'Open', so we went on through into the small office building. There was no-one behind the counter. I poked my head into the hallway—nothing but a small bathroom, and an untidy room full of stacks of paper and a folding cot with a rumpled blanket.

"Looks like Jim's been spending nights here," I said to Kevin. "No sign of a dog."

At the back door there was a button with a sign that said 'Ring for service.' Kevin considered it, and shook his head. "Just in case there is something going on here, it might be best if we don't announce our presence too loudly."

All I could see from the back doorstep was a gate in another fence leading to rows of concrete block buildings with metal doors. There wasn't a clear view in any direction due to the haphazardly arranged piles of building materials and junk everywhere.

"We'll find him faster if we split up," Kevin said. "If you see anyone, just yell, or blow your whistle." He went left and I went right, weaving my way around various heaps of salvaged material of dubious value. I turned sideways past a stack of plastic birdbaths and some seriously tacky garden gnomes. I was developing a suspicion that Jim was more of a hoarder than a successful business owner. Mid-row, my route was blocked by an avalanche of broken photocopiers and I had to pick my way with care.

I was getting even hotter and more irritable with the idiot who'd called us out here and then disappeared without so much as leaving a note when I realized there was a better way of doing this. This part of the Salvage District wasn't crowded with people. I should be able to use my psi-abilities to zero in on one lone man. I gave myself a mental kick in the butt for not suggesting that at the start. I'd been letting my annoyance with the job override everything else. That wasn't how a field agent should behave.

I stepped back into the meager shade of a pile of tires and let down my shields, questing for signs of life nearby. There was Kevin, his shields an irritation like a pebble in my shoe, off to my left. And to the right, a faint trace of something unfamiliar. I lowered all my shields, straining to make sense of that elusive trace, and then everything went fuzzy. My feet seemed to start moving of their own accord, drawing me to the back of the lot.

Behind the back row of storage units were a couple of dilapidated metal garages, and more piles of junk too big to fit in the units. And some good-sized trees. Tall oaks and maples, clustered close together. Despite the bright sunlight I couldn't see the fence behind them. It was darker than it should have been under those trees. One had grown up right through the roof of a garage. The door was halfway up, buckled and twisted.

"Holy cow", I whispered. "That's a Grove." These trees could spring up full-grown overnight after a magic storm. And things got weird around them. People who went into the trees didn't always come out again. Jim should have gotten a woodcutting crew onto this right away before the trees got any bigger.

Protocol dictated I should have gone to find my partner at that point but I couldn't seem to think clearly. I knew I just had to go a few steps further, and I would find something wonderful. I stepped around the corner of the garage and stopped, stunned.

Their heads were down in the long grass, but I got occasional glimpses as they moved about. These were definitely not lost ponies— their coats were such an intense white in the spring sunshine that it almost hurt to look at them. They were the size of a thoroughbred horse, but shaped more like a large antelope. Long snaking tails with a big tuft of white hair at the ends swished languidly. Both beasts sported a single straight golden horn that looked nearly two feet long. Unicorns! I'd actually made first contact with a mythical species!

I was grinning like an idiot. This was my big break. No slip-ups now, I needed to document this properly. I slipped my camera out of my bag then focused on the nearer of the pair. They both appeared to be grazing, but they were sure going to town on that vegetation, wrenching and tearing at it. It seemed a rather violent way to eat grass. Maybe they were pulling it out to make a nest?

I heard a clunk from behind me.

"CJ!" Kevin whispered urgently. The unicorns stopped moving, heads up. Perfect.

Click.

The larger of the two unicorns sniffed the air. His tapering muzzle and beard were plastered with red. Maybe he'd been eating berries.

Click.

Kevin gave up on trying to be quiet.

"CJ!" he hissed. "We need to get out of here!"

I ignored him. Stupid elf. I had to get closer. They were so beautiful. Dreamily, I let the camera hang from my neck and walked toward them, my hand outstretched. The smaller unicorn was watching me with interest, ears pricked forward. I took another step forward to stroke her velvety nose, and something squished underfoot. Everything seemed to go into slow motion at that point.

I looked down at what I'd stepped on. *Oh,* I thought sluggishly, trying to process what I was seeing. *That must be Jim. And those are his intestines.*

The unicorn lunged at me, teeth snapping. Somehow I had time to note that those were not the teeth of an herbivore. I got a sudden rush of mental images from her, and then there was a terrible pain and I was flying backward.

Kevin had grabbed hold of my harness and yanked me backward. The mare skidded on the red mass in the grass, recovered her footing and came at us, the stallion right behind. Kevin dragged me around the corner of the garage.

"In there," he yelled, giving me a shove. I fell to my knees and crawled under the buckled door as the unicorns rounded the corner. I looked back and saw both unicorns stop and recoil from him, ears flattened. Kevin dived under the door and yanked on it from the inside, managing to get it most of the way down. He flipped over a table, dumping the contents on the ground and propped it against the gap.

Outside there was an angry squeal and then the impact of a large body slamming against the door. I took one look at my hand then slid down the garage wall. There seemed to be a terrible amount of blood there. Distantly I could hear something whimpering like an injured animal and realized it was me.

Kevin rummaged through his pack.

"Hold still," he said, and crouched to wrap a pain amulet around my wrist. My hand went numb. I almost passed out with relief.

"Here, let me see it," he said, laying out the first aid kit.

I was trying not to look.

"How bad is it?" I said.

"I think you've lost the top finger joint of your ring finger. But the good news is you still have your middle finger, in case you need to flip anyone off," he said, swathing my hand in gauze. "Here, try to keep your hand upright."

I took a deep breath. The thought that a piece of me was now inside that unicorn made me want to heave.

"I always wanted to get my name in the Mythological Index," I said shakily. "I just didn't expect it to be as a unicorn snack."

"What on earth were you thinking, trying to pet it?"

"I lowered my shields to try and find Jim." I looked down at my red-stained boots and swallowed hard. Another pair I wasn't going to want to wear again. "They've got extremely strong mind powers. Suddenly I really wanted to be as close as possible to them, to touch them. Maybe even go for a ride."

I shook my head, disgusted at my own carelessness, then looked at Kevin.

"They didn't affect you at all?"

"I can assure you I did not feel the slightest urge to ride a unicorn, pet a unicorn, or braid ribbons into a unicorn's mane," Kevin said with great dignity.

I suppressed a giggle. "That's a shame. You'd look so lovely together."

Reluctantly, he smiled. "They are beautiful, aren't they?

"That glamour must be how they catch their prey. Animals just stroll up to them and wait to be eaten. Interesting that they're not affecting you. Are you wearing a mind-shielding amulet?"

His smile thinned. "Not exactly. Given what my family is like, I've had a great deal of practice at resisting Influence."

I'd been thinking that DROCA was no place for an elf. Belatedly it was occurring to me that there were probably other people who thought that too, and weren't shy about letting him know it.

He'd put himself between me and the unicorns, giving me time to get under the door. Maybe I'd been reading the elf all wrong.

"Your folks didn't name you Kevin, did they?" I said suddenly. Kevin looked at me like I'd started spouting gibberish.

"Are you feeling dizzy? You've lost a lot of blood there."

"It was a perfectly sensible question!"

He snorted and gave me a mocking bow. "Celebrimbor Telperinquar, at your service, ma'am."

"Wow. That's a terrible thing to do to a little baby."

He shrugged. "My folks are into the whole elven heritage thing."

"Anyway, thanks for saving my life back there."

"You're welcome," Kevin said. I think he might have been blushing but it was hard to tell in the dim light. He turned his back on me and picked his way past the tree growing through the middle of the garage.

"Hey, looks like there was some sort of hydroponic setup back here," he called back. "I think Jim was growing fire weed." I could hear him rummaging behind the tree.

"I was wondering about that," I said. "That Grove has to have been here for more than a week judging by the size of it, but Jim only called DROCA yesterday. He must have wanted to move his growing operation before any agents saw it. Given the amount of stuff piled up around the place it probably would have taken him a week to clear out a unit."

"Maybe the unicorns got here through the Grove, somehow." He bent down to check on my hand and I remembered something.

"They reacted differently to you."

He wouldn't meet my eyes. "Maybe that part of the legends about unicorns and virgins is true."

"You?" I couldn't believe it. The guy could have been a super model, if we still had such things. "You mean you've never—not even once?"

"I'm asexual," Kevin said firmly. "And that's all I want to say about it."

"Huh. Good to know. Did you get the impression they might let you past them?"

"Not really. I think it was more like I smelled bad. I think they'd still happily run me through if they worked themselves up to it."

There was another crash from the door as something hit it. The back end of a unicorn, I suspected.

Kevin got up to look down the back of the garage on the other side of the tree.

"Hey, there's a side door here!" I heard a click and then the door slammed shut again.

"I found the other unicorn," he called, sounding a bit breathless. There was a crash as something hit the door next to him.

"Excellent detective work there." I got up carefully, trying not to jostle my hand and picked my way past the tree to join him. My eyes had adjusted to the dim light now.

"Do we really need to get out of here right now?" I said. Slam! The door shuddered under a mighty kick.

In the distance, a bell began to ring.

Kevin sighed. "If some idiot should stroll out here looking for Jim—."

"Then we're knowingly endangering civilians," I finished for him. "Is there anything here that we can use to fend them off?"

Unfortunately this was the one place in the entire yard Jim had kept tidy. Trying to produce a clean product, I guess. There was the hydroponic equipment, a tangle of old sheets used as dust covers, some buckets, and about twenty grand worth of harvested fire weed.

Kevin got down on all fours to look under the table. "There's some fertilizer here, a toolbox, and some oil." He dragged it all out. "Do you think they're afraid of fire?"

"It's a long way to the gate," I said. "How about we slow them down a bit first?" I waved a hand at the crates of fire weed.

"You think it'll affect them?"

"I know it will have some effect on them—I just don't know what, exactly." That was why fire weed was illegal—not because it would get you high as a kite, but because the effects varied wildly according to the amount of magic in the area and who was taking the drug. One hit and you might get a high that lasted for days, or drop dead on the spot, or be immediately plunged into psychosis. That's why one of the drug's street names was roulette.

After a few minutes work, I was crouched by the main garage door, wearing the respirator from my field kit. Kevin ran back from the side door.

"Ready?" he said, and I nodded. He began setting alight the buckets stuffed full of fire weed and shredded sheets lined up next to me. I took the smoking buckets and tossed them out under the gap, one-handed. I waited, counting to fifty in my head. There was a lot of snorting going on outside. Cautiously, I lowered my shields and reached out for a brief check on the unicorns. The fuzzy images I was getting back made me grin.

"It's working!" I whispered to Kevin. We moved quickly to the side door. He lit the torches he'd made and I opened the door a crack. Nothing. I risked sticking my head out. The buckets he'd tossed out this door were filling the air with smoke but there was no sign of the unicorns. We dived out the door and ran, zigzagging down the aisle of junk to the other side of the lot, then turned right toward the office, ears pricked for the sound of pounding hooves behind us. I hoped there was enough steel in the junk piles around us to act as a unicorn repellent.

At the end of the row we came face to face with two men and a boy, and skidded to an abrupt halt. From the other end of the row I heard a snort, and a crash as a unicorn staggered into a junk pile.

"Run!" Kevin yelled at them but they just stood there gaping past us at the oncoming unicorn. Nulls, I suspected. Probably wouldn't recognize a DROCA agent if they ran up to them screaming and waving a flaming torch. Their minds were completely defenseless. I flicked an image at them of the first thing that came to mind: hairy black spiders the size of cats suddenly streaming out of the junk piles toward them. That worked a treat. They all started yelling and running, shoving each

31

other in their haste to get away. Kevin neatly headed them off before they could run right past the office and directed them through the gate. I brought up the rear. I turned back in the gateway. The mare had stopped thirty yards away. She was surveying the surrounding piles with quick nervous glances. I stubbed out my torch in the dirt and shut the gate, grinning. Fire weed could make you very suggestible.

Inside the office I flopped down on a chair for a minute. My finger had bled through the bandages and I was feeling rather lightheaded. Kevin was on the phone, and there was no sign of Jim's customers. They were probably still running. It felt like I'd only shut my eyes for a minute before he was in front of me.

"The department is sending out a full Containment team. They should be here in half an hour," he said, winding a fresh pain amulet around my wrist. "Everyone sounded very excited."

I opened one eye. "Lovely. That gives us time to write up our report."

"I'll take care of that. And you know what, partner?" Kevin said, grinning at me. "I insisted they send a car out, just for you."

I gave him a weary grin in return. "Thanks—partner."

**S.A. McKenzie** is a writer of offbeat and blackly humorous science fiction and fantasy stories featuring time travelling rabbits, carnivorous unicorns and man-eating subway trains, because someone has to speak up for these misunderstood creatures. Find her online at www.hedgehogcircus.com.

# Three A.M. Challenge
## by David Powell

Air conditioning saturates the house with white noise. The wee, empty hours hold me suspended when all I want to do is start the day. I can't stop cycling through all I have to do before my nine o'clock tomorrow. Check the laptop, update the stats, feed the girls breakfast, drop them at two separate schools, fight the traffic to mid-town, coach the team, crush the presentation. Superdad scores corner office.

Beneath the AC hiss, a soft chant begins.

*I leave for you this body, please take it.*

*I leave for you this body, please take it.*

I crack open my bedroom door. Orange light wavers on the wall opposite Keisha's room. I shrug on my robe and tiptoe down the hall. Keisha's reedy, nine-year-old voice chants steadily.

*I leave for you this body, please take it.*

I peer around the door. Keisha sits with her back to me, erect, arms folded on her desk, a lit candle in front of her standing between two mirrors. They intensify the candle's light, make my daughter's shadow dart and swerve on the walls.

*I leave for you this body, please take it.*

The chant sinks into my stomach and freezes. I step forward and see Keisha's fingertips resting on a homemade doll. Burlap twisted

34

into arms and legs. Mismatched button eyes, red gash of mouth stitched up with black thread.

I resolve to keep the alarm from my voice.

"Keisha, sweetie, it's awfully late."

She continues to chant.

This is not Keisha behavior. Her dolls are cloyingly cute; she doesn't go for the homemade ones. She never stays up late, either. She goes at life hard, then sleeps like a rock as soon as her head hits the pillow.

*I leave for you this body, please take it.*

The room wobbles with occult chanting and wavering shadows.

What if she's sleep walking? Isn't it supposed to be bad to wake them? I can't remember if I heard that from a friend or read it in one of the parenting blogs I study like scripture. Trying to keep informed, to be not just a good dad but a *smart* dad. My database of parental wisdom is suddenly blank.

Fighting a panicked urge to grab my daughter and dash from the room, I place a hand on her shoulder. I will not yell. I will not issue ultimatums.

"It's a school night. You should be sleeping."

She sighs and looks up at me.

"The YouTube girl said it has to be now, Dad."

\#

My ex-wife Lilian and I promised ourselves, once we admitted we had little but contempt for each other, that we would *not* raise our girls in a toxic environment. It wasn't the girls' fault our lives had taken separate paths. We agreed to share custody in the most constructive way. We would:

> 1) Never speak ill of the other in front of the girls;
>
> 2) Never fish for information about the other's social life;
>
> 3) Never withhold crucial information; and
>
> 4) Listen, listen, listen to what the girls have to say.

Not prying into each other's social life was easy, because we were both too busy to have one. Day to day practices were trickier. Things like when to permit junk food, and how much internet time to allow, for example.

But internet *time* was the least of it. The world they entered when they logged in, that was terrifying. We leaned heavily on her sixteen year old sister, Zoe, when her school began shooting us those alarming emails. We gave Zoe the third degree about gaming and sexting and neo-Nazis. She was remarkably calm and reassuring. The school didn't know what they were talking about, she said. This was old news. Just because a kid in Texas killed herself didn't mean everybody was doing it. No one bullied her or Keisha. No human traffickers were luring them in. We felt supremely proud that our daughter had such common sense.

Then that bitch in Lilian's knitting club showed her Zoe's Instagram. There was Zoe, ripe and inviting. Wearing a bra with no shirt, painted-on jeans shorts we didn't know she owned. Worst of all, gym shorts and no top at all but her forearm.

Just seeing the picture put me in a tailspin. I was mortified at how many seconds it took me to hit delete.

Worst of all, she didn't get mad or try to defend herself. Just said, "Okay, I'll take them down."

Lilian said right then we were beaten. No way we'd ever catch up to her. Like the high frequency ring that teenagers can hear but adults can't. I sat Zoe down to ask about it.

"What about this ring only teenagers can hear?"

She smirked, thumbed at her screen.

*Call me back real quick.*

When the phone lit up with Marcie's name, Zoe's brown eyes shone with devilish glee. She held her phone up to my ear and I could barely hear it, faint as an insect buzz from the next room. The summons of her tribe, swirling around her deaf old man.

#

Transfixed by reflected light and dancing shadows, I back into the hall. My skin prickles, the same uncanny sensation I had listening to the ring. Phantoms I can't see or hear fill the air. Drawing my girls in, shutting me out.

Zoe stands outside the door in lacy silk shorts she shouldn't be wearing and her pentacle tee shirt. Five words surround the star: courage, strength, integrity. She hugs herself and I can't read the other two.

"Put some clothes on if you're cold," I say.

She's watching her sister and doesn't respond.

*I leave for you this body, please take it.*

"Do you know what she's doing?" I keep my voice calm and level. That's one thing I can do that kids can't, keep my cool in the grip of strong emotion. Well, not really. That used to throw Zoe off balance; she does it better than me these days.

Zoe shrugs.

"It's all over YouTube, kids trying to scare themselves. Called a 'Three a.m. Challenge.'"

"Uh *huh*. Challenge to what?"

"You do this ritual and a spirit or demon or something's supposed to possess the doll. Then you can make it do things. Or so they claim."

"What kind of things?" I try to relax my jaw, because I'm grinding my teeth.

"Well, last week she did this to scare Mom into buying her a neon unicorn."

"Last *week?* Dammit! Lilian said nothing about this."

Zoe sighs and puts her head to the side, exactly the way Lilian does when I can't remember how the wash cycle works. The room crowds with things I don't know. More invisible phantoms.

"Did she learn this from you?"

I know that's unfair. I know my voice is shaking. Well, so what? I've got maybe two more hours to sleep before we hit the ground running. Like I can sleep after all this! If my presentation falls flat, three people are lined up to bulldoze me out of a raise. Lilian's dinky-ass trainer job won't pay two mortgages! These damn girls need to understand all we're doing for them.

Am I in charge of this house or not?

I stride into the room and stand over Keisha, fists on hips. She keeps her eyes on the candle.

"Dad, you can't interrupt it."

"Oh please, by all means. Finish it! Do it exactly the way you're supposed to. Let's see how well it works!"

#

Six a.m. Daylight an hour away and the whisper of traffic from the connector already rising to an impatient hum. I sit on my bed in half lotus, meditating to make up for loss of sleep. Rather, intending to meditate. You're supposed to accept all thoughts without judgment, to let them come and go, but my thoughts won't go. They squeak and gibber and collide like bats trapped in a closet.

Lilian has betrayed me; our co-parenting agreement is shredded. How much have they hidden from me, she and the girls? How much has the internet corroded my daughters' innocence and undermined my authority? How ready are Casey, Rashaun, and Harsh to jump in if I blow the presentation? Buzzing around the office like bees, fetching my coffee, quoting their favorite business blogs. I'm already too white and conventional for the promotion track. Add in sleep deprived, angry, and guilt-ridden and I'm just one more failed divorcee waiting to be downsized.

A scratching sound punctuates the AC hiss. It's coming from Zoe's door. Keisha is locked in there with her sister, at my order.

I try to regulate my breath, waiting for the scratching thing to find my open door.

That's what you do, Keisha said. Wait for it to find you. If it fails, don't go hunting for *it*. It might mess up your house, but if it thinks you blew the summons, you're marked. Marked is very bad. Everyone despises a failure.

Who made up these rules? Where does this entity come from? Some homespun voodoo backwater, some Appalachian *haint*? The invisible world is infinite; I have to admit Lilian taught me that. You need a discipline, a system of procedures, to navigate it. All the more reason for her to tell me our daughter is calling up some *thing* she found on the internet!

I rub my thumb along the ribbed sphere of the brass object in my hands. It's warming up. The scratching thing has its attention.

The thing is moving now, rasping along the skirt board like a blind person in unfamiliar territory. So why the button eyes? Don't they work? Good thing the mouth is sewed up; I'm spared a voice, at least.

It stops at my door and faces me, silhouetted by the hall's nightlight. A burlap homunculus, wobbly on its new legs. It points one stiff little arm in my direction. That was the signal, Keisha said. It was mine to command.

Maybe I should just command it, then. Go throw yourself in the trash. Pet the cat and let it tear you to pieces. Set yourself on fire.

But no. No telling what animates this thing. Too many uncertainties.

"Stand still," I tell it, raising the vajra. Ancient brass, triple pointed on either side of the sphere. Ebay is one good thing about the internet. Saved me a trip to Tibet to get this artifact, the genuine article. Five hundred dollars; Lilian threw a fit. Stuck away in my bottom drawer like the last pack of cigarettes, just in case I…just in case.

I hold it by the middle, clawlike points exposed, and say the words:

*Lady of Trauma, Lady of Pain*
*Pull me from the disaster I have made of my life*
*Save me from the evil machinations of others.*

A beat, a pulse radiating in all directions, a blurry wave that touches the doll and sends it up—*whoosh*—in a burst of green flame.

*Yes! Still master of the house!*

My smugness lasts only seconds, the time it takes the blurry wave to reach the girls.

#

Lucky. Lucky. How are we lucky?

Lucky the garage is attached to the house, so neighbors can't see us bundling Keisha into the car, can't hear her keening.

Lucky it's keening now, not the ear splitting, spine ripping screams of a few minutes ago.

Lucky that Zoe's secret stash of her mother's magic isn't used up. Enough blessed linen remains to wrap her sister's fingers.

Lucky Keisha's fingers are mangled, not severed, and Lilian's house is just two blocks away. Zoe makes the call to make sure she's home.

I shake with the effort to drive normally, not screech out of the driveway and burn rubber.

"Sit up, like we're just going to school," I say, though I doubt the girls hear it.

The Lutons are out on their lawn in the gray light, bending over something on the grass. Bebe looks up as we pass. Her face is drawn, distraught. The black heap on the ground must be Coco, their poodle. The one they don't even try to keep from shitting on our lawn.

Zoe puts her phone to my ear.

"What did you use?" Lilian's voice is scratchy and clipped. I want to scream at her. *This is your fault!*

"The vajra," I say through clenched teeth. "Why didn't you tell me Keisha was casting spells?"

She breaks the connection. Shit. Here we go. She'll sue for custody now, surely. I can't wait to see the wording of the complaint.

We pass the club house. They barred my girls from the pool all summer because I objected to the neighborhood covenant. Windows are shattered. The pool fence is ripped apart like paper.

"Dadeeee," Keisha pleads, sobbing.

Lilian's garage door is open. She stands just inside in her Oiselle shorts and pullover, hand on the keypad, watching us pull in. Panting, interrupted mid-run. She signals to wait till the door closes completely, then we're a flurry of motion. All business; no talking. Zoe pushes the car door open and slides her sister across to me. I scoop her up and Lilian is there unwrapping the red-stained linen, uttering a small *hmph* of judgment.

The flesh of Keisha's fingers is peeled back from the tips to the middle knuckles, little bananas of blood and bone. Bone which looks, thankfully, intact. She tries to move them and gives a small cry like a kitten that wants in the door.

"Don't sweetie," Lilian says, with a gentleness that pierces me because I haven't heard it in so long.

We stumble down the basement stairs, falling into accustomed roles. I light the candles. Zoe places the soiled linen into the basket woven from hawthorn branches, branches Lilian and I cut on our honeymoon to England. We'd been giddy with love and mischief, giggling over the lengths we went to, smuggling the sacred wood back to the states.

Lilian croons an incantation to calm Keisha, then turns to me.

"Did you bring it?"

I pull the vajra out of my pocket and show her. It's wrapped in two pot holders bound together with a rubber band, but still alarmingly hot.

She asks how I used it.

"I invoked the Trauma Goddess."

44

"With this thing, because?"

"Vajra is thunderbolt, unstoppable; and diamond, indestructable."

Her lips purse and contract with the effort to keep from yelling. I know what she's thinking. *You never studied Vajrayana! You can't pick and choose power objects like a buffet!* Maybe she'll yell later, when Keisha is out of danger.

More likely she won't. She's done yelling at me.

I turn to the herb cabinet but Zoe has already gathered the jars. She glances at me and then quickly bends to her work, expertly whittling strips of sandalwood so thin that light passes through them. She pauses to tuck her hair behind her ears; it's auburn and straight, like mine. Keisha has hair like her mom. It sticks out like a reddish, frizzy dandelion.

Lillian cradles Keisha's head as we ease her inside the drawn circle. It's smaller than I remember. They've adapted the practice to my absence. I'm just in the way.

"No men allowed for the rest of it," Lilian says. I have to admire the control in her voice.

"I know."

I recall how I suffocated in this clannish circle, but I still feel abandoned.

Lilian should have told me about Keisha. *She should have told me.*

"Could you please go to the drug store?" she asks. "We'll need first aid afterwards."

"I'll call the schools, too."

"Thanks."

How can so many layers of irony fit onto a single word?

#

Morning traffic has swelled like flood waters in the past half hour. Even if I left for work right now I'd be an hour late. Twenty minutes creeping through traffic lights to the first parking space I can find, two blocks away from the drug store. I weave through the crowd on the sidewalk, droopy-eyed people with their coffee, bearded homeless hard at the day's begging.

A firetruck blats and bullies its way through traffic. Two cops are at the corner blocking off this street. Three doors down from the drugstore an empty lot gapes where the vape shop stood, the one we tried unsuccessfully to run out of the neighborhood, because they sold candy-flavored oils to our kids. The front wall and pulverized interior are sprayed on the wall of the apartment building behind it. It's been flicked away like an ant at a picnic.

I stop with the rest of the gawkers, stumble back with them as the firefighters set up a perimeter. What good can they do? There's no fire to put out, just a granular mish-mash of concrete, glass, metal, and plastic. Are firemen trained for disasters like this? What's the process for response to the inexplicable?

The right tool for the right job, my dad always said, but his expertise ran to re-building carburetors, hanging doors. He lived in a mechanical universe. He owned four sets of drill bits, but had nothing to say if his children were angry, or sad. No advice beyond "That's not real," when nightmares boiled out of us. Lilian had refreshed my psyche like a cool drink of water. She showed me the invisible forces all around us. They could be persuaded, nudged, placated.

My questions amused her at first. "Why stop at Wicca? Why just one set of tools?" Over time, as I read on my own, the same questions made her defensive. She resisted more aggressive practices, didn't want to accept how dangerous the world could be. She refused to see the need for weapons, but I wasn't living in a sylvan cottage. I was clawing my way up the corporation.

On impulse I pull out my phone and open maps. There. My flag waits beside the vape shop that still exists in cyberspace. I widen the view. My shopping district, my neighborhood. I drop a pin at my house and trace a line from there to the Lutons, to the club house, to the vape shop. All places I owed a grudge. I pull out to include downtown. My office stands right in the path of the wave, if it's still going.

I punch my office number and get Peg, my assistant.

Her voice shakes. "Thank goodness you're all right. Casey, Rashaun, and Harsh are in comas. Looks like they spent the night in the office you're sharing."

Busy little bees. Of course they did.

"Corporate is scared it's Legionaires or something," Peg says.

She tells me not to come in. CDC has put the building under quarantine.

#

On the last day of kindergarten, Lilian caught Keisha cramming all her school-manufactured art into a trash can.

"But sweetie," Lilian held up a popsicle stick dream catcher, its yarn half-unravelled. "It's your *first* art."

"It's just like everybody else's."

"I think it's *beautiful,*" Lilian crooned. Keisha gave her the look that says *beware, crazy bag lady.* Both girls give her that look whenever she overdoes the positivity. I'm pretty sure they learned it from me.

"It *could* be beautiful," Keisha said. "It could be *amazing*. If you'd let us, *you know*."

Because we haven't let them, *you know*, they've found their own ways of getting what they want. It's not like they need magic to get around us, anyway. They call each other with rings we can't hear, pass along spells on YouTube. They don't worry about discipline or tradition. Here's a thing you can do. Okay, let's try it.

Lilian would say I'm the same, but more reckless. Okay, so I used a nuclear weapon on a flea. The point is I found a nuclear weapon. So what if I never studied Vajrayana? I could. I could study the hell out of it. I'll get the promotion now. I'll be head of my division, hire whoever I want, even move my office to Tibet if I feel like it.

Sirens continue to punctuate the morning; disasters little and big are being discovered, in an expanding circle radiating from my house. Waiting in line at the drug store, I pull the bundle from my pocket and unsnap the rubber band, tracing the weapon's lines with my thumb. It's warm, no longer hot. I'm itching to watch the news, to know how far the effect goes. How many miles? How many rude drivers, disgruntled waiters, smug divorce lawyers, suspicious insurance adjusters? How far down the pissed off scale does the wave travel?

A slight tug at my thumb, a hitch, like a yo-yo string at its limit, declaring its intent to glide back to my hand.

To return.

I dash to the door, pushing shoppers aside, skirting the firemen's perimeter. Force my trembling hand to unlock the door, wrench the car back into traffic. Swerve to avoid side-swiping a car and clip another car's bumper, cut down a neighborhood street out of the morning rush.

The dashboard clock says seven forty-eight. Less than two hours for the wave to return, if it travels at the same speed. A yo-yo speeds up on its return. Doesn't it? It can. I don't know. Keisha knew what her doll would do; I don't have a clue what will happen next.

I should warn Lilian and the girls.

No, I should keep driving, get as far away from them as possible.

Thunderbolt is unstoppable. Diamond is indestructable. Family is fragile as glass.

**David Powell** writes full-time in Georgia, seeking out the little pockets of chaos that hide in the grid. He is a member of Horror Writers Association and my work has appeared in Shotgun Honey, Calliope, Oklahoma Pagan Quarterly, and HWA Poetry Showcase Volume 6.

# The Magnificent Hat
## by Bethany A. Perry

The guy inside the door, his face filled with more scars than whiskers, except for his incredible eyebrows, scowled at me until I closed the winter back outside. I dipped my head at him, my throat tight. The question I asked myself as I loosened my scarf in the hot pub was if I thought I should scurry or hold my head high.

My body ended up picking something in between and I kind of hunched and slunk my way to the bar. The only seat was right between some pale burly man with a mustache like a limp caterpillar and a gent who still had every stitch of winter clothing on, including an impressive wide-brimmed hat with a peacock feather flourish tucked into an intricately-braided band.

I scrunched myself between them, trying not to touch either and failing. My sleeve caught the well-dressed fellow's scarf and I accidentally pulled it away from his mouth. Head cocked, he reached a gloved hand up and readjusted it.

"Sorry," I muttered, easing my rickety stool closer to the bar. Teeth clenched, I waited for him to get testy.

Instead, the wide brim of that glorious hat tipped, and he turned back to his drink.

I exhaled, abs still tight, and removed my own dinky hat.

Caterpillar Mustache grinned. "Don't mind 'im. E's still salty about the job we did yesterday."

"I'm sitting right here, Virgil." A voice issued from Magnificent Hat and though his scarf covered his mouth, his words were clear as bells. Not muffled at all. "You don't need to speak as though I can't hear your great, bellowing voice."

Virgil chuckled, mustache bouncing. "Figured you hadn't dug the wood out of your ears lately, Bob-o. It's hard for you, what with yer—"

Bob-o spun. Between the brim of his hat and the scarf, flinty eyes peered out, seeming to pierce Virgil with a glare. Firelight from the lamps flickered over them.

The heat radiating from that stare almost scared me off the stool. I swallowed and tried to make myself small, sorry these two idiots didn't just sit together instead of making me think there was some kind of island of safety at the bar, and waved to Henry, the bartender.

He sauntered over without a word and thunked a tankard of ale in front of me.

Equally loquacious, I slapped two silvers on the bar. One for the drink, one for the man. It's always a good idea to keep your bartender happy.

With a nod, his dark brown head void of hair, he slid the two coins into his apron and disappeared down the bar. Not before scowling at Virgil.

"His panties are too tight," Virgil said, speaking into his ale. Like he wanted someone to hear, just not the bartender.

"Maybe if you weren't such an asshole." Bob-o sipped his drink. Some splashed over the side, wetting his glove.

Grumbling, Virgil turned away from them both and watched the rest of the pub.

I'd been in here before when it was like a pub had broken out in the middle of a party, but for some reason the crowd was subdued tonight. Maybe it was the cold, but no one spoke above regular volume. Even the people playing cards pitched their voices low and played with something like calm patience.

The hair on the back of my neck prickled. Everyone seemed so calm, and I was only halfway done with my cheap, watery ale, but the atmosphere made me want to bolt. It started with Bushy Eyebrows over by the door and just got worse with these two. But my intuition had been made fun of more than once, and I was not about to fall into that trap again. I'd sit here and finish my ale if it killed me. I turned to Bob-o.

"So what do you and Virgil do, Bob-o?"

He shook his head. "Robert."

Flummoxed, I shook my head back.

He chuckled. "Don't call me Bob-o. Only Virg gets away with that. Call me Robert, please."

I expected him to put out his hand and ask for formal introductions. But he saved me the trouble of lying about my name and kept his hands to himself.

With a shrug, I drank a little more, getting closer to the bottom of the mug. Henry sauntered back over to put away some clean tankards.

"Hey Hank," I said, leaning over the bar, "quiet in here tonight. What's going on?"

Virgil turned just a bit back towards us.

Henry shrugged. "Don't ask me, Wil. I just work here."

"Wil, is it?" Virg leaned over. "Let me buy you a drink."

I shook my head, his mustache bearing down on me, his breath hot in my face. Suddenly the full pub was too much, the smoke in the room closing in on my lungs. My skin shrank from his touch as he threw an arm around my shoulders and laughed.

"Wil, you can be my new best friend." He shook me, rattling my teeth. "Bob-o can be a real jerk, you know? Got a stick up his ass."

And he laughed so hard at that, his pale face turned red, the laughter guffawing from his mouth and right into my ear. He stopped breathing in the middle and just kept wheezing, arm around my shoulder tightening as tears popped from his eyes.

"He's not wrong," a soft voice whispered in my ear.

Mouth open, I started to turn, even though Virgil and his floppy mustache bounced in my face and his arm pulled me back and forth. Why was Robert pushing me into him, hemming me between the two of them?

It was that moment I figured out what they did for a living.

Robert slid off the stool, flipped a silver to Henry, and sauntered out into the night air.

My coin purse in one hand.

***

Rather than follow him, I sat for several hours and made friends with his partner. Virgil turned out to be loud and obvious but also surprisingly witty and generous with free drinks.

He could afford to be, considering he was clearly spending stolen money. I almost felt bad drinking with someone else's money but it takes a lot of Henry's ale to really start feeling it, and I had come in here to drink anyway. I always had that limit, the line I couldn't afford to cross, but I didn't get close to drunk before Virgil was slurring his speech and forgetting what day it was.

Henry's wet cloth squeaked over the bar in front of me. "It's late, Wil. Don't think I've ever seen you out so late. You OK?"

I nodded, eyes on Virgil as he stumbled through the empty pub, the card players and low-talkers having mostly packed it in for the night. Considering he was now losing a fight to a coat rack that wouldn't release his jacket, I could probably steal back more than what Robert had taken from me before he slipped out into the freezing night. It'd be like fleecing a sheep. Virgil would never even know what happened.

So I slid off the stool and followed him out into the icy air. I wiped slushy, half-frozen ale from the hair glued to my upper lip as he rounded the side of the pub and disappeared into the alley behind it.

I peeked around the corner.

Virg leaned against the building, swaying a little, and hummed to himself as piss warmer than the air around it steamed onto the paving stones beneath his feet.

Shivering, I wished it was that easy for me to take a piss in an alley. Goddamn nuisance, taking a piss.

Unsheathing my small blade, not much more than a dagger, I crept closer as Virgil leaned against the building and started snoring. It was a shame he wouldn't be awake for this. I slipped my glove off my right hand. I hated doing that, I always felt like my hands were a giveaway, but I needed my fingertips free to get at his coin purse.

My slender hand stole into his coat.

"Helping Virg get back to the inn?"

I jumped, ran into Virgil—who snorted and smacked his head into the wall—and spun.

Robert the thief stood behind me, scarf pulled across his mouth. But I heard the smile in his voice.

I stammered. "He was um. I just."

Virgil leaned on the wall and grinned, one corner of his mustache in his mouth. "You were going to rob me, weren't you?" He shifted on his feet, hand on the haft of his shortsword.

That was it. Cornered in this stupid, freezing alley, breath a puff of smoke in front of my face, the stench of Virgil's warm, ale-stinking piss in my nose, I'd had enough. These two had robbed me, point blank, in front of the whole pub, and now threatened me when I tried to get back what was mine. I pointed my blade between them, backing up. "Only because you already stole from me, Bob-o. Stole everything I had, didn't you?"

He stepped towards me. I hadn't noticed in the pub, I'd been too busy fuming about my coin purse, but he had an awkward, wooden kind of gait. Like one of his legs was stiff, maybe arthritis in the knee or an old broken bone. Something I *had* noticed had been the rapier hanging at his side, and now he drew it, waving it in front of his face and settling into a dueling stance. "Want to fight me with that pig-sticker, Wil? Think you can get close enough inside to make a difference?"

My head swam. Something put me off about the way he spoke, about his face, but I couldn't put my finger on it. And he was right. My knife versus his sword was a terrible match-up for me. So it was either swallow my pride and starve for the next few days until I got paid, or see if I could hop inside the range of that rapier and get to him before he got to me.

With a sideways grin, I squared my thin shoulders and raised the knife. "Try me, Bob-o."

A loud exhale issued from him and he waved his sword again. "I could be mistaken, but I thought I asked you not to call me that."

He lunged and I almost missed getting out of the way because I had discovered what the problem was with his face. There was no cloud of breath in front of it. Even after that exhale, when the cold night should have produced what looked like dragon's breath, there was nothing.

But I did get out of the way and he spun like a top on a pin, swinging at me with an economical little swipe that nicked me on the shoulder.

As he finished the swing, I pushed all my weight to the ball of my foot and leapt in, past the edge of the rapier, and aimed my knife for his shoulder. Not only did I want to repay the warm blood spilling inside my coat, I didn't want to *really* hurt him. I did kind-of like him, thief or not.

He danced away and my blade almost missed.

But with my smaller stature and the secrets hidden in my coat and trousers, I had to have an accurate swing.

My blade never missed.

And it didn't this time.

It cut through his coat like butter and must have sliced through all his skin and muscle the same way because it clunked like it had hit bone.

He hissed and jumped back, raising his blade again and lunging toward my stomach with the tip.

My own blood, still warm and steaming as it left my body, splattered him as I swung my knife and parried his blow.

But he didn't bleed from the shoulder wound. Not a drop.

Before I could raise the blade to come at him again, Virgil grabbed my bleeding shoulder and shoved me back. I cracked my head on the wall and saw nothing but white. The ale still laying in my stomach wanted to come back up.

I clenched my teeth and swallowed it back down, the back of my throat burning.

Virgil stood next to Robert, checking his arm. "You're OK, buddy. Just a little notch."

My swimming head tried to catch onto just what in the hell Virgil was talking about, because "notch" didn't make a bit of sense. But my stomach still rolled and I was probably lucky I hadn't passed out.

Robert's scarf had come down again. His expression stiff, he glanced at his shoulder and readjusted his coat. "It's a scratch." But his mouth didn't move when he spoke. It didn't move at all.

I held my head. Hallucinations, now. Maybe I should sit down.

But Virgil advanced on me. "You could have really hurt him. He don't heal like you and me. He—"

"Hey hey hey, what's this?"

Holding my head, I tried not to turn too fast.

Henry stood in the back door to the pub, a barrel of trash under his arm. Framed in the light spilling into the alley, he looked like not much more than a large, dark blur. His muscled arms bulged with the strain of carrying the large trash bin. His expression inscrutable, he stepped further into the alley.

"Doesn't concern you, barkeep," Virgil said, stepping towards him.

Now that Henry was out of the light, I could read his eyes a little more. And what they said was "duck."

I did.

He dropped the bin on the frozen paving stones and lifted his arm. The voice that issued from his mouth was one I'd never heard from him. It was deeper, and it echoed. "*Magicae telum.*"

Something like a fast wind blasted past me, rippling the skin on my face. Another wave rushed almost directly behind it and it was a good thing I was down low already because its wake knocked me on my ass.

But what it did to Virgil and Robert astounded me.

They both flew.

Fifty feet down the alley it blasted them. The energy waves must have hit them both square in the chest. Robert's fine hat flew off and landed in a slushy puddle, maybe even someone else's alleyway outhouse. He landed with a boneless thump.

Virgil, on the other hand, sat up as soon as he landed, laughing so loud dogs started barking. He crawled to Robert's hat and brushed it off, chuckled, and crawled back to Robert, who still hadn't moved.

I had to blink a few times because when Virgil lifted Robert from the ground, Robert only bent at the waist and it looked like he wasn't breathing. But as soon as Virgil settled his hat back on his head, Robert gripped his side.

"Ow. What happened?"

A voice came from the mouth of the alley. "Fighting in the streets is illegal, boys. Looks like it's a night in jail for all of you while you sleep it off."

Stomach sinking, I followed the voice to its owner.

Three members of the constabulary, weapons drawn, badges shining in the dim light coming from Henry's back door.

Great.

***

Henry and I sat on a wooden bench, facing bars almost wide enough for me to slip through. Almost. The window behind us was a tight, glassless rectangle, also not big enough to slip out of but small enough to keep most of winter outside.

*Ffflllpppttt.* Our one guard shuffled cards by himself at the end of the hall, out of sight.

A small blessing in this total cock-up of a night, they didn't strip search anyone coming in. That saved me a lot of fast talking. They did take our weapons and do a half-assed pat-down. I guess being three in the morning made everyone tired.

Speaking of tired, Virgil lay, spread-eagle in the floor, snoring.

Robert sat on the only other bench, one leg crossed over the other, tapping his hand on his knee. Every few minutes he'd stare at Virgil and sigh, swinging one leg. His face still mostly hidden by the shadow of his hat, I just had to imagine his annoyed expression based on his posture and all the sighing.

I leaned my head toward Henry. "Thanks for helping me out."

He shrugged. "I've always liked you, Wil. You don't cause trouble and you always tip." His dark brow furrowed and he narrowed his eyes at Virgil. "I thought somebody was ripping off my customers, just didn't know who."

Virgil snored.

Robert leaned back against the wall, drawing his hat further over his eyes. "Your customers are easy marks, Henry."

"You keep talking, I'll show you a lot more than what you saw in that alley."

I turned to him. "What was that, anyway? I've heard of magic, was that what it was?"

He shrugged and opened his mouth.

Robert chuckled. "Yes. Now that we've established that…" He trailed off and stood. Hobbling, he walked to the bars and leaned against them.

"I didn't know you could do magic, Hank." I bumped him with my shoulder, my cheeks hot. A real spellcaster and I'd known him for years. "I've never even seen magic done." A wide smile split my cheeks.

He grinned, lips parting to show bright white teeth I hardly ever got to see. "How do you think I keep the peace in my place?"

I shrugged. "I thought it was the bow and arrow you kept under the bar, to be honest."

Robert sighed again and limped away from the bars. "You've seen it. You just didn't know you had." He reared back and kicked Virgil in the ribs. "Get up. It's time."

Virg snorted and sat up, wiping the side of his face and mustache with his sleeve. Copious amounts of drool soaked into it.

Force of will kept me from gagging.

He coughed a few times, sucked some air in through his nose, and spat a giant glob of something I was sure I didn't want to think about into the corner of the cell. "Guard gone?"

Robert nodded, shifting his hat with one hand. "He's gone to take a piss. We've got maybe two minutes."

"Then what are you talking to me for? Can you reach it?"

I watched them move to the bars, bickering like a married couple, and wondered if their plan included me and Henry. It was their fault we were here in the first place. I opened my mouth to say so, but Robert reached through the bars and swiped at the wet mop sitting next to our cell. After some fiddling, he backed up with it in one hand. "If you put me on this thing wet side up, so help me—"

"I ain't gonna do no such—"

"Already landed in a puddle of piss tonight, you daft fool. I don't know why you didn't just leave the pub sooner."

"Are we gonna jaw till the guard comes back or—"

"Can't even trust you to properly steal some coin—"

Virgil grabbed the mop with one hand and Robert's hat with the other. With an unceremonious tug, he jerked the hat off Robert's head.

Robert fell to the ground like a sack of potatoes, accompanied by a hollow *thunk*.

I stared, mouth open, as Virgil pushed his arm through the bars and settled the hat on the mop. Wet side up.

He let go of the hat and the mop.

It stood on its own and turned to him.

And then it spoke. "I told you not to put me on the wet side."

Robert's voice. It was Robert's voice speaking.

I glanced at the pile of arms and legs in the floor.

Henry threw his hands in the air. "You've got to be joking me."

"Wh— Um. Wh—" I couldn't spit any words out.

The mop hopped away, Robert's hat perched on top.

Virgil turned around, arms crossed, and leaned against the bars. He smiled. "Any minute now."

I stood. My legs like jelly, I collapsed back onto the bench and stared at him. "Wh—"

"What's going on? Haven't you figured it out yet?"

The mop hopped back to the front of the cell, wood handle thumping against the stone floor. "You're lucky this mop is easy to manipulate." One of the strands on the mop-head held a small dagger, its wet end wrapped around the haft and dripping grey water onto the floor. "Too bad you're terrible at picking a lock. The key went with the guard."

With all the ferocity of a wild dog, I latched onto the thought of doing something useful. I stood again. "If you need a lock picked, look no further. It's one of my specialties." I drew in a breath and held it. I'd get out of here without them, probably in the morning, but jail made me nervous in a way I wouldn't explain to them. "But you have to take me and Hank with you if you're escaping."

Virgil started to shake his head.

Robert *tskd*. How he did that without lips, I have no idea. The simple fact that somehow he was able to transfer his essence to the mop through his hat was just. It was just.

What kind of weird night was this turning out to be, anyway?

"Virgil, I am standing here on a wet mop with piss all over me and you want to turn down the only one in this cell who can pick a lock? What, did you learn how in the last five hours?"

Without a word, Virgil took the small dagger from Robert— from the mop—and handed it to me.

66

The handle, still wet with mop water, pressed into my palm. I dried it on my pants leg and leaned into the bars. This, of course, brought me quite close to what I could only call a sentient mop that stank of mildew. "Uh. Hi Robert. Is this magic, too?"

"Pick the lock. We'll have a nice, long chat about it later."

I worked the dagger into the huge lock on the outside of our cell door and got to work. It was difficult with just one tip and I wished I had my whole lockpick kit, but the guards had taken that along with my weapons.

The first pin fell and I began to work on the second, also using the blade to hold the first one up. This was the trickiest part.

And as if it wasn't bad enough, the door at the end of the hall swung open.

Virg hissed under his breath. "Bob-o. Company."

The mop spun.

The mop spun as though there was a face on the front of it where the ragged wet strings hung down.

I almost lost my grip on the dagger.

But I didn't, and I focused on the lock as though a living mop wasn't fighting our sleepy guard at the end of the hall, and as though it hadn't just swept his legs from under him with just the stick end.

The guard fell to the floor with a meaty thump.

Something I just realized had been missing the two times I watched Robert take a fall. No meaty thump, just a woody crash. Like a pile of sticks had been thrown to the ground.

Leaning over me, his breath still boozy, Virgil spoke into my ear. "Do you almost have it?"

The final pin fell and the door swung open.

Virg grinned, one chipped tooth in the front digging into his lower lip, and stepped out of the cell. "Someone help Bob-o."

I stood like a lump in the middle of the doorway until Henry prodded me in the side with one pointy index finger. "I've got him. Let's go."

And indeed, he had the boneless lump of person that had, until recently, been Robert under his arm. Carrying him like an empty keg. "Go, Wil. Let's go."

I rushed from the cell.

The mop had cornered the guard, who was backed into a literal corner and shaking. I guess he hadn't seen magic until tonight, either.

Virgil advanced on him. "Where is our stuff?"

The guard glanced up at him and his face hardened. Like now he had a real enemy he could fight and he seized the opportunity. He squirted past Mop Robert and dashed toward Virg, trying to pull out his police stick as he did. It seemed to be stuck in its holder.

That didn't stop Virg from punching him in the face.

But the guard was wily and bounced back from the punch like it was nothing. He slipped under Virgil's reaching grasp and wrapped his arms around Virg's waist.

I thought Virgil was going to the stone floor but he was steadier on his feet than I realized. He backed up into the wall, one hand on each of the guard's wrists, and twisted his hips, bringing one knee up.

Fascinated by his agility, I almost forgot what we were doing.

"Wil, grab our stuff," Henry said. "Especially my pouch there." He gestured with the hand not holding Robert's limp body.

Following his pointing finger, I found a rack of cubbies against the wall. The front was barred and locked, but all our belongings were just behind the small lock.

I gaped at him. "I've got nothing to open this with! I need the key!"

Virgil and the guard continued to fight, the guard too wily for him to grasp for long and Virgil too agile to be knocked down. Virg panted, his mustache puffing out with each exhale like a little flag on the front of his face.

Henry pushed past me. "Stand back."

As I watched, mouth open, Henry gripped the lock in one huge fist. He spoke a few words under his breath and furrowed his brow.

Sweat popped out on his upper lip and he groaned, squeezing the lock tighter. He shook his head, mumbling, "I can't, I can't, I can't."

But it looked like he could. An odor of burning Sulphur and a wisp of smoke floated away from his clenched fist. I waited for the peculiar scent of charred skin and prepared to pull him away from the lock before he hurt himself.

With an exhale, he squeezed tighter. Something crunched inside his fist. He opened his fingers and what was left of the lock tumbled to the ground in little pieces. Some of it ash. He lifted a brow and glanced over his shoulder. "Gonna need a nap after that one." Pawing the cupboard open, he grabbed his sack and half the weapons. "Get the rest of this stuff."

I did, just as Virgil finally went down with a great shaking.

And, of course, several more guards showed up in the door. Looked like our guy wasn't here alone anymore.

The mop had spent the whole time hopping around Virgil and shouting like he was a cornerman. When the other guards came in, he jumped up and rammed the wooden end of his handle into the stomach of the first guard.

The guard went down with a woof and the hat fell off the mop.

Both lay silent in the floor.

I scooped the rest of the weapons and belongings into my arms, noting that I had gotten Robert's coin purse.

Excuse me, *my* coin purse.

I skittered to the hat and scooped it out of the floor.

Virgil popped up, holding his head, and squared up to the guards coming in the door. They just kept coming. At least six of them.

And three of us. And none of us had empty hands.

I couldn't use any weapons while I was still holding this hat.

So I put it on.

Vertigo was a word for it.

Transportation to another plane of existence was another.

Whatever it was, I'd never felt anything like it. My ears were plugged, my sight blurry, my voice when I said *what the hell* came from so far away I could hardly hear it. It was like an invisible sheath had been slipped over me, separating me from the world and sensation and everything that was going on. I couldn't feel my fingers.

***

*Hey, Wil. Thanks for picking me up.*

Who is that?

*It's me. Robert.*

I don't understand. What's going on?

*We don't really have time for this. We're outnumbered. I won't last in jail.*

71

Neither will I.

*Ah, yes. Just like me, you're not only what you appear are you? You're more.*

I… yes. You could say that.

*Well, Wilhelmine, if you'll help me, we can get out of this in one piece. Haha.*

Are you a ghost?

*I'm a hat, Wil. I'm a hat.*

A magic hat?

*No. I'm a person, a regular person, but now I exist as a hat. Long story, but I can animate whatever I'm on. Like the mop.*

Your body is a mannequin. That's why you move like you're made of wood.

*Now you're getting it. If you let me help you, we can get out of this together. What do you say? Teamwork?*

You stole from me. Why should I help you?

*For the love of the gods. If you help Virgil and I get out of this, I'll pay you back and then some. Deal?*

\*\*\*

What choice did I have?

\*\*\*

Shoving all the rest of the weapons into my left elbow, I gripped Robert's rapier in my right hand and spoke aloud. "OK. Now what?"

Pins and needles rushed down my arm. It flopped away from my body, the rapier flying into the air. I attempted to steady it, concentrating on my own elbow as it bent in a way it really shouldn't have, and struggled to work with whatever this magic was, rather than against it.

*Stop fighting me.*

"Sorry," I said aloud. "I'm trying."

*Relax. Look out!*

Without another thought, I ducked and backed away from the door. The space where my head had been was suddenly full of someone's fist.

I let my arm go limp, trying to just let it be Robert's conduit.

The pins and needles lessened and instead what felt like a rush of warm water flowed down my arm. Loose and easy, I gripped the handle of the rapier and took a swing at the guard coming for me with his shortsword extended. One easy deflection later and I kicked him on the way down.

With a grunt, he smacked his face on the floor and lay still on the stone, moaning.

*Spin.*

I did what Robert asked and my arm flew out on its own, slapping another guard on the ass with the flat side of the rapier. He stopped chasing after Henry and whirled around, baring his teeth at me.

But the rush of triumph I felt in handling the rapier and Robert's commands at the same time was more than he could take away from me in one flash of his teeth. I was handy with a blade myself, but Robert was *spectacular*.

We danced around the room, the two of us working in perfect, symbiotic harmony, and rounded up each of the seven guards with ease. By the time we were done, the guards sitting in a tight circle inside the cell, Henry and Virgil had put down their loads and simply applauded.

Without thinking, I removed the hat to take a bow.

I staggered and dropped the rapier, the empty feeling of Robert's absence immediate.

Chuckling, Virgil teased the hat from my slack fingers. "I think we should oughta get now. We'll carry ol' Bob-o till we're outside. He can't run too good with those wooden legs."

Giving him a weak smile, I picked up the rapier and followed them out the door.

74

\*\*\*

The golden sun cleared the horizon, working its way up to our faces as we sat on the south hill, staring over the town. Morning kissed the rooftops, glowing pink and spreading along the streets.

Virgil sighed. "Heck of a night, buddy."

Robert, back on top of the wooden mannequin, nodded.

I sat between Robert and Virgil, snatching glances at Robert's face. In the sunlight, with his scarf and everything removed, I could clearly see that his face was stuck in one expression. Though I had to wonder why he chose mild surprise. Maybe I could get him to change his eyebrows a bit. Look more intimidating.

He handed me back my coin purse. "Think you've earned that."

"Thanks." I stuck it in my inner coat pocket.

"We're gonna need a new job, Bob-o." Virgil reached in his own coat. With a flourish, he pulled out and unrolled a map. "Check this out. It got mixed up with my stuff in that jail." He blew on it, and dust flew into his face, catching in his mustache.

I took it and held it up.

Robert leaned over and scanned it. Something like a whistle came from him and for a moment, his expression of mild surprise fit. But he shook his head and leaned back on his hands. "Virgil, we don't have the resources. And even if we did, we don't have the manpower."

I turned my head back and forth to follow their conversation, cranking my neck as the lumpy ground put one awkwardly-folded leg to sleep. It was so obvious they were fishing for volunteers from Henry and me that I wondered how long I could let them go on without laughing.

But Henry beat me to it. "Ain't got time for you to beat around the bush," he said. "You got me arrested outside my own pub and now I'm a fugitive along with you idiots. Not only that"—he sighed and crossed his arms—"it's gonna get out I use magic and that never ends well. I'm coming with you."

I supposed there was no getting around it. Besides, teaming up with them had thrilled me down to my core in a way my life hadn't in years. I couldn't let these three leave town without me.

Before I could volunteer too, Robert spoke again. "There's something I must tell you two about Wil."

I held my breath and considered fighting Robert's pronouncement. But I didn't know how I'd go about that without drawing attention to myself. How would Virgil and Henry react to the fact that I—

"He is the best fighter I've ever had the pleasure of working with and if the time should come again where someone has to wear me, however temporarily, I ask that it be him and only him."

My breath leaked out from between tight lips and my stomach filled up with butterflies. A smile stretched my lips before I could even

76

think about it. "Robert, that's the nicest thing anyone has said to me in ages." I stood and stuck my hand out to help him up.

Virgil clapped me on the back, hard enough to run me into Robert. "A great treasure awaits us, gents!" With a grin, he strolled off the hilltop. Henry followed.

Still holding Robert's wooden hand, I leaned close. "Thank you."

He tipped his extraordinary hat, the peacock feather ruffling in a slight breeze. "Looking out for each other is what we do. Welcome to the family, Wil."


**Bethany A. Perry** is a southern transplant in the west, where she's made her home with her kids, partner, pets, and several hostages…er…houseplants she hasn't killed yet. Poetry was her first love, and she's been writing since she could hold a pencil. Horror is her sweet spot, but all things sci-fi and fantasy are also deeply entrenched in her heart. Find her at http://www.bperrywrites.com

# The Prisoner's Cage
## by Alex Minns

He hit me again. I wasn't sure if the stars I could see were from concussion or the sparks dancing round his hands. I hate fighting electrical mages.

The roar of the crowd washed over me. They had a renewed vigour at seeing me go down; they could smell blood. Figuratively anyway. Although it wouldn't have surprised me to see a few vampires in the throngs. The idiot I was fighting decided to strut around the cage, rattling on the wire mesh and roaring at his fans. The shouting got louder as they all pressed in closer. Faces were twisted into snarls, both men and women alike, baying for blood. It wasn't the classiest of crowds but, as magical martial arts were banned by the Council, you weren't ever going to get the high-flyers.

A bare bulb hung overhead by a single wire. My opponent swatted at it, doing a good impression of King Kong. The light blinded me for a second until it passed, swinging back and forth repeatedly. Shadows swayed around the cage. Kong turned to face me again, the moving light playing on his face, turning him into some grotesque flick book.

He advanced, to the delight of the crowd. Sparks intensified around his fists. Kong was an apt nickname. He was built like a brawler; meaty hands on the end of thick arms. He wasn't tall but he was broad. And as I had discovered, solid too. He closed in, grinning, before gripping my throat and lifting. My legs scrambled underneath me as I fought to stop my head snapping backwards. The stench of sweat and burnt hair clawed at my nose as I gagged for breath. White energy danced across the man's eyes as the charge built up within him. Whatever he was about to unleash was going to hurt. I steeled myself, tried to draw my senses inwards but something distracted me. I wasn't even sure what, but something nagged at the back of my mind. It wasn't Kong. My eyes flicked past him towards the crowd and scanned the people. They all blended into a mass of seething limbs and venom. The further back I looked, the darker it was. But there. My gaze tracked back. Two people who didn't fit. Behind the crowd was a tall, shaven-headed man and a woman with hair tied back and arms folded across her chest. She was frowning as she watched the cage. I squinted, aware of the pressure building around my throat and the pins and needles that indicated his growing charge. I tried to push the feelings aside for a second and focus on the woman. I took as deep a breath as I could and slowed my heartbeat down, making the world slow down with me buying me a few seconds. As the sounds dulled to a distant throb, I focused on her lips.

"He's not what I was expecting." There was a pause. "Well, he's losing for a start." Time snapped back to normal and the lack of air getting through to my lungs drew my attention back to Kong.

"Not so cocky now," Kong snarled. His other fist hurtled towards my face. The two in the crowd had distracted me and I didn't manage to brace in time. My head snapped back and hit the cage wire behind me. Blood pooled in my mouth. My nose wasn't broken but I was going to have a lovely black eye in the morning. "Your friend lost his cockiness too." I thought back to the pictures of Solar's body out by the river. "The best bit about this cage. No rules, no consequences." He drew his fist back again; the white sparks were jumping violently away from his hand. The crackles and pops drowned out the noise of the crowd. "Once I've finished with you, maybe your lot will stop poking around in Kristoff's business."

"Kristoff?" The question came out as a hiss, blood collecting at the back of my throat.

Kong's brow knitted in confusion and his grip relaxed a little.

"You work for Kristoff?" I managed a bit more this time. "Solar was more of a business rival. So, Kristoff has the files." Kong started to growl. He still hadn't figured it out. When people think they have the upper hand, they start talking too much. Normally, I try and get more information but the pair in the crowd were bugging me. Kong's hand round my throat tensed, telegraphing his next move. His other fist opened as he prepared to unleash electricity straight into my face. I took another deep breath and slowed my heart rate. The crackle became slower as I raised my right hand and pulled back on his thumb. The pressure on my larynx dissipated and I sidestepped to my left pushing Kong's left arm away from me and opening up his body. Now I was safely out of the range of his targeted electrical discharge, I brought my right knee up into his midsection and relaxed my grip on time around me. A split second of confusion registered on Kong's face before my knee connected and he doubled over, smashing his head into the cage. The noise of the crowd dulled for a second as they all reeled in surprise at the turn of fortunes.

Kong recovered quickly and spun, spittle trailing from his mouth. His face was now set in a grimace as he realized he'd been conned. I allowed the next few seconds to play in my mind, seeing what his next moves would be. I needn't have bothered; he was fueled by blind rage. He lurched forward, attempting to charge at me. I spun out of his way and used my momentum to grab his back as he passed me and throw him into the opposite wall. Instinct took over my body and the next few moves came fluidly without me needing to think. In thirty seconds, the crowd had fallen silent. In forty-five, the match was over. Kong was lying on the floor of the cage, breathing but unconscious. I stepped over from his prone form. The announcer entered the cage and declared the match over. Grumbles and complaints echoed round the audience as money changed hands. I moved over to the door and climbed through the small gap, grabbing the money from the weasely guy waiting there but my eyes were on the pair still standing back from the rest of the crowd.

Bodies retreated as I made my way through the masses. There were a few angry grunts thrown my way by people who'd lost a fair bit of money but no-one blocked me. I ignored them all as I weaved my way through, heading straight for the pair. The woman looked startled by my direct approach; she kept looking to her companion and then back at me. He on the other hand, looked almost disinterested. I could see a haze of yellow in his eyes. Great, a fire mage.

I walked directly towards them and veered at the last second to skirt round. I glanced over my shoulder as I paused.

"I need a shower and I'm not talking out here." I didn't wait to see if they responded. As I made it to the door to the changing rooms, Marty gave me a knowing look and glanced pointedly behind me. So they had followed. I gave him a discrete nod to let them pass and kept marching. I breathed a sigh of relief as the light hit me. The fighting floor was so dingy and full of shadows it gave me a headache. When you can see time move, it helps to have the proper light to do it by. Poor lighting always made my brain ache. The bright clinical lights in the hall to the changing rooms were a breath of fresh air and the soundproofing helped too. As the door closed behind me, I was given a second of blessed relief before my two new friends followed in. I led them through the corridors to the main locker room and headed straight to mine. No-one had spoken yet. I figured the big guy was trying to size me up and psyche me out. I just hadn't figured out what had brought them to me yet. They were either representatives of someone I'd annoyed, or they had a job. He looked like I'd annoyed someone, but she looked like she had a job. I caught her nervous glances in the reflection of the mirror on my locker door and locked eyes.

"It is rude to stare like that."

Colour-me-surprised, I hadn't expected him to speak first. I grabbed my towel and turned to sit on the bench.

"Funny," I replied, "seeing as you were staring and talking about me while I was fighting. And you questioned my ability." I pointed at the woman. I expected her to back down, let her nerves take over but instead she cocked her head and looked intrigued.

"You read my lips? Is it your temporal ability that allows you to do that?"

She sounded like a scientist. I reassessed her and decided she needed closer watching than I'd first thought. In fact, there was something decidedly familiar about her. As I narrowed my eyes, a wave of panic flushed her face and she stepped back slightly.

"You clearly know who I am, but I don't know who you are. Or why you're here?"

"We have a job offer." The man stepped forward, partially blocking my view and access to the woman.

"I don't listen to offers from people I don't know." I waved my towel at him dismissively.

"It is not from us." The big man produced a phone out of nowhere. He hit one button and I heard the dialling tone.

"Is this supposed to intimidate me? Or impress me? 'Cause if I'm honest, it's a bit too nineties cinema for me. Don't get me wrong, I love films but..." The ringing ceased as the call connected. He held the phone out to me. I stared at him. He stared back. I could tell he was not a man used to folding and I really didn't want to sit here all night. With a roll of my eyes, I snatched the phone out of his hand.

"Hello, do you deliver within the hour? I'd like two ham and mushroom pizzas…" The laughing on the other end of the phone made me stop. I knew that laugh.

"Remi, you better be being nice to my people," the woman's voice drawled, oozing with confidence, which in my experience was well earned.

"Well if it isn't Her Majesty herself. When the Witch Queen herself sends her goons, I know I must be in trouble." The woman in front of me snorted indignantly. There was seriously something familiar about her. The hair was wrong though.

"Ooh, you did not just call Helios a goon. And you're not in trouble. I just need a favour."

I could picture her as she spoke, laying across some sofa as her minions ran around her organising every black-market deal in London and undoubtedly further. A flick of the wrist and they would all bend to her every command, and if they didn't, her magics could make them bend, if not snap, under the strain. She was not a woman to be messed with.

"I don't owe you any favours," I pointed out. "And the last time I did you a favour, I ended up with a run in with Council

Enforcers, two different angry gangs coming after me and only half my pay."

"The only reason it was a run in with enforcers rather than an execution was because I stopped them, I took over those angry gangs so they stopped harassing you and you got more than your fair share once I had to account for paying the damages you caused," she countered. It was true. I'd broken a lot. And she really had ousted those gang leaders. I knew full well it was a consequence of the job that she had been fully anticipating. That was the real reason she put my back up, there was always another angle.

"Still don't owe you a favour." My mind whirred through all the chatter I'd heard recently and then it clicked. I leaned back against the cool metal lockers and smiled. "However, the bounty on Little Miss Victor here would definitely be a nice bonus, just in time for Christmas."

The man, Helios she'd called him, stepped forward, eyes blazing.

"You will not touch her." Queen's voice hardened, taking even me by surprise. I'd seen this woman do some twisted stuff but I had never heard anger so quickly.

"And I'm not touching this job either. I'm not getting involved with Council fugitives. Nice to catch up but…"

"You haven't heard the payment yet."

I took a deep breath Don't bite, my brain screamed, don't bite. "What's the payment?"

"Castigan."

I sat up a little straighter. "I'm listening."

"I need an extraction. The Council are holding a person we need to help prove that there are some very bad men pulling the Council's strings, Castigan being right there with them."

"Castigan is an Enforcer now. He's untouchable. If I take him on, either I die because he kills me or I die because the Council execute me."

"You get the man we need, you won't have to face Castigan to ruin him."

She let the silence hang between us, knowing the turmoil she'd caused. The two in front of me were almost motionless as if worried they would break the tension. I let my hand lower and looked at the phone. I hung up. She didn't need to hear me say it, although she would have loved to.

"Who are we breaking out?"

####

"Well this changes things." I lowered the binoculars and passed them to Helios. I leant against the side of the car, peering over the roof towards the building.

"These are nice," Helios mumbled. I couldn't help but smirk.

"Don't listen to whatever Queenie says, I am a professional. And being professional means having lots of toys." It also meant always being out of pocket but I kept that one quiet.

"Professional what exactly?" The fugitive, Miss Victor, stood at the other end of the car, her arms still folded across her chest. She had been keeping her distance from me since I'd identified her.

"Jack of all trades some might say. I'm an extractions specialist."

"A mercenary." Her tone was accusing.

"Mercenaries are guns for hire. I retrieve people; some who need rescuing, some who need capturing." I pushed myself off the car and moved closer to her. I saw Helios stiffen. To be honest, Victor wasn't what I'd been expecting. Kezio Constantin was the main man on the Mage Council, a real big hitter with serious power. This slip of a thing had put him in intensive care? Black magics, however, were not to be messed with.

"And who tells you they need capturing?"

"Whoever's paying." I threw her my best lopsided grin.

"A mercenary then." She paused; her gaze flicked to Helios before coming back to me. "Like Castigan."

I was moving before I realised. Helios was between us in an instant, his hand on my chest. He looked like he wouldn't be able to move too quickly, more muscle than finesse but he held himself like a coiled spring. No, he would be harder to take down than he looked. But not impossible if it turned out to be necessary.

"I am nothing like Castigan." Even I could hear the hatred in my voice. I had to crane my neck to peer round the bulk of Helios. "What did the Witch tell you exactly?"

"Nothing," Victor shook her head. "I just heard her say his name on the phone and suddenly you were on board. I know he was a mercenary before he became an enforcer so..."

"And what about you? Queenie has never associated so openly with enemies of the Council. Can't believe she'd take on a black mage that the Council wants to string up. The bounty I'd get for you."

"Back off," Helios warned.

"See! He wants the money and doesn't think to ask why my bounty is so high. Do we really need this guy? We can get in and out of there," she had moved beside us and was staring at Helios.

"No, we need him. Just as he needs us." He leaned in closer. "Keep taunting her like that and I will see to it that you do not get your five minutes with Castigan." He took his hand away from my chest and stepped back. "Now, can we get back to the task at hand. There are many more enforcers down there than we anticipated." He waved towards the warehouse.

We were parked on an area scrubland that had a high vantage point over the warehouse. The bushes kept us fairly concealed but thankfully this was a public track through the nearby fields so we could explain away our presence if needed. The man Queenie wanted was in the warehouse on the left, where the highest concentration of enforcers was. There were probably no more than fifteen of them but seeing as this was a Council-run facility, they would all be mages and fifteen would be plenty enough.

"Why is this guy so important? I've never seen the Council put up such a show of force for just one person."

"They must have gotten word that we found out about him. Emily won't be happy someone talked," Victor screwed up her face.

"Emily? The Witch Queen's name is Emily?"

"She's going to be annoyed at me isn't she?" She looked at Helios who didn't respond except for the tell-tale flicker at the corner of his mouth.

"You still haven't told me who he is," I pointed out. Victor stared at Helios, obviously the big man was in charge here.

"The man in that building is called Lee Baxendale and he has evidence we need." Not at all cryptic. I raised an eyebrow and continued to stare at him.

Victor broke first. "The Rebellion."

"What rebellion?"

"Exactly." She grinned at me as if she'd just scored a major point. Helios let out an exasperated sigh.

"You know, you're not like other black mages I've met."

Her eyes flashed angrily. "I'm not a black mage. I didn't do it."

"Uh huh, practising that one for your trial." It was just too easy.

"They set me up, framed me. Your mate Castigan is the one that attacked Constantin, and we can prove it."

"Then why don't you? Give your evidence to the Council"

"Who do you think ordered Castigan to do it?"

A cold feeling crept down my spine. I'd heard rumblings of power shifting in the Council for a couple of years, but there are always rumours. I'd have completely dismissed them if it weren't for Castigan. It had never made sense him going over to be an Enforcer. It was the antithesis of him. And yet he had signed on the line, selling me out in the process. The man had no morals, no loyalty, no scruples. He was no enforcer. But a heavy for someone controlling the Council, to do their blackbag jobs? Yeah, that sounded like him. "Someone is making a play on the Council?"

"They've already done it. The real Constantin died. We don't know who the man wearing his face is but he really doesn't want us to get to Baxendale."

I leant against the car again. No wonder Helios hadn't wanted to say much to me. This wasn't just an extraction. This was an act of war against some shadowy take-over of the Mage Council. They were the law and government for all mages, not just in England but across the world. If the heart of the Council had been corrupted, that wasn't good. But it also meant acting against them put one hell of a target on your back. Common sense told me I should walk away from this.

But Castigan.

If they were happy to use him to get rid of their obstacles, who knew where it would end. He'd come looking for me eventually. I looked back at Miss Victor. She definitely didn't look like a black mage. She didn't look much of a threat at all really.

"What did you do?"

Her shoulders slumped and she looked down to her right, almost embarrassed. "I did research. I was a Council archivist. They thought I'd found out about something I shouldn't have."

"What?"

Helios shrugged and pointed towards the warehouse. "That's why we need him."

I pulled the binoculars out of Helios' hands and surveyed the scene again.

"Haven't they got some thermal bit that can see through walls?"

I looked at the woman with exasperation. "Thermal imaging can't see through walls."

She looked away, her body crumpling in on itself again and she took a few steps away mumbling, kicking at the dirt on the floor.

"Right." I moved round to the back of the car. "Well we have no idea where he is in that building so it's best I go in alone."

"How do you figure?" Helios followed me. Victor had lost interest in what was going on and was staring off into the distance. I caught Helios' gaze and nodded across at her. He watched her for a minute and tilted his head in understanding. There was no way an archivist would survive the melee this would quickly become.

"I move faster than they can react. Can't take you with me. Faster I get in and locate him, the better. Once I do, it's going to get noisy quick, at which point, I could do with a diversion and an exit route. That's you." I started rummaging in the car and found a small black zip up case. I pulled it on top of the other boxes and opened it up. I pulled an earbud out and slid it into place. Wiggling my jaw helped me get over the weird sensation. I motioned for Helios to help himself to another set as I wrapped the throat mic around my neck and flicked it on. I turned away so I could test it and saw Victor peering round me to see what we were doing. I hesitated, wondering whether I should offer her a set but she just raised her eyebrows and nodded before wandering over to the other side of the car again.

"She is not used to any of this." I heard Helios directly in my ear. "It has only been six weeks since she discovered the Council framed her."

"You going to be alright with her or should we get her to wait up here?" The best thing about the throat mics were you barely had to speak to be picked up. Victor was three metres away and completely unaware we were speaking.

"We will be fine." He sounded confident but as I watched her pulling at the edge of her sleeves, I wasn't so sure.

"Once I leave, give it six minutes before you get into position and have a diversion ready."

"If Castigan is in there…" Helios began.

"Castigan isn't the job. We extract the target, get him back to Queenie and then we settle with Castigan."

I pulled out my favourite toys from the back of the car. It was loaded with all kinds of awesome but in a pinch I always went for my trusty tools. My escrima stick was forged by a powerful mage who imbued it with protections and the ability to cut through other magics. It also gave a good whack to the head when needed. I slid it into the custom holster I made for it; I'm a man of many talents. My modified taser went on my other hip. It was another mage design; this one had a cartridge that allowed five shots and worked even once disconnected from the gun. I caught Helios looking at it enquiringly. I knew that look.

"I don't kill people. Absolute last resort and even then," I shook my head. The number of people I had killed was in single figures but I still remembered every single one of them. All but the first had been a kill or be killed situation. The first one still keeps me awake at night. "The electrical charge disrupts even the strongest mage from gathering their energies. This keeps 'em down for fifteen minutes at least. Right, I'll be off then. Help yourself, but don't break anything yeah?" I left the boot open and made my way round the car to the edge of the bushes. Victor cast me a sideways glance.

"Good..."

"Don't, never say that," I held up a hand to stop her. "Ever." She shrugged and went back towards Helios. As I pushed myself into the claws of the foliage, I heard her speaking over Helios' mic.

"He's weird."

I smiled. I was growing on her.

#####

"You've got two men coming round the corner from your left." Helios' voice crackled in my earpiece. I was still at the edge of the bushes. There was a six-metre gap between me and the warehouse wall, plus another two metres to the metal staircase up to the fire exit door on

94

the first floor. It was possible to make it in time, assuming the door was unlocked. I ground my teeth together.

"There's movement from your right too, think they're about to meet in the middle."

Decision made, I took a deep breath and closed my eyes, willing everything in my body to slow before pushing the feeling out around me. I didn't wait to see if it had worked. I launched out of the bushes and into a flat-out run for the staircase. The men would hear something but the time distortion would make it impossible to figure out. I took the stairs two at a time not caring about the clanging. I focussed on keeping my breathing steady, I couldn't hold time back forever: from the moment I started, it was fighting back against me, like running through mud. I smashed into the door and grabbed the handle. I paused crouching down before I tried; if there was someone waiting on the other side, I didn't want to be directly in the firing line.

The door edged open and I slid my head into the gap. It took me a second to adjust to the lack of light. I didn't sense any motion so slipped inside as quickly as I could, pulling the door shut. I collapsed into a heap as I let go of the moment.

"If you're going to move Remi…"

"I'm in."

"You are? Oh, right. Good luck."

"Don't... oh for." My teeth ground together. I took it from Helios' comment that I had made it in unnoticed. Once I had my breath back under control, I took in my surroundings. There were benches scattered over the place with electrical points hanging from the ceiling. Bits and pieces were scattered everywhere but they were covered in a layer of dust. It had been a long time since this place had been working. Slowly, I rose from my crouching position and started to inch forward, holding my breath for the first few steps. As I got further, my confidence rose. The floor spanned the whole length of the warehouse with a central staircase running in the centre as well as another at the opposite end of the floor. There were a couple of rooms off to my left. Noise drifted from the staircase but I wasn't close enough to know if it was above or below.

A scraping noise drew my attention towards one of the doors to my left. I was vaulting over the nearest table before the door was fully open. My feet slapped on the floor as I ran the last few steps making the person behind pull the door open wider to look. But I was already on him. I kicked the inside of his left knee so he dropped and started to spin round. I grabbed at his neck and held him tightly, restricting his air supply and stopping him from calling out. Once I felt his unconscious body go limp, I dragged him back in the room, hoping I wasn't about to find a room full of other enforcers. Thankfully, the room was empty. I pulled a ziplock tie out of my back pocket and secured the man to the pipes in the corner of the room, far enough away from the window so he couldn't attract attention when he came to.

I checked my watch; I'd already lost two minutes and I hadn't even located the target yet. I hurried my pace and made for the stairway at the end. The noise was coming from the lower floor. I had no choice but to go down the first couple of stairs to get a look at the layout. There were six enforcers just in my eyeline. Fifteen had been an underestimate. A man and a woman were at the opposite end by the main entrance. Three more enforcers, one woman and two men, were sat at a small table set up in the middle of the space. There were more rooms off to the right. The nearest room was set up as a makeshift kitchen. But it was the one room to my left that was odd. It wasn't an original feature, that much I was sure of. It seemed like a single box had been built in the warehouse and there was one enforcer sat right outside the door. Well, I'd bet my gran's dog that the target was in there. It was metres away but the only way in was through the door the enforcer was sitting at and I was fairly certain any movement would attract the attention of the three at the table. I needed to wait for the distraction.

I sighed and checked the clock: ninety seconds until my six minutes were up. This was not great. I should have had the target by now and been ready to exit. I still had to break him out of the box and as I looked closer, I spotted markings scrawled on the outside. Now when a teenager on my old estate scrawls something on a wall, you call it graffiti and ignore it. When a mage scrawls on a wall, you sit up and make bloody sure you know what it means before you do anything about it. I cursed under my breath. I was about to centre myself when a loud explosion buffeted the whole warehouse. Even the stairs I was perched on seemed to shake. The reaction was immediate. The three at the table rushed to the nearest window and the two at the door went outside. They shouted to each other, one pointed at the man on the box who nodded and stood firm. Why couldn't he have gotten curious? It was Helios' fault, why did he have to wish me luck?

I took a deep breath trying to shake off any tension and slowed down. When I felt the resistance, my eyes flicked open and I leapt over the stair railing. I could see the enforcer notice me in slow motion. His head started to turn in my direction. I was too far; even slowed down the man had time to defend himself. I saw a shimmer of blue start to crackle in front of him as he willed a barrier into existence. I never stopped running. My hand went straight to the escrima in the holster and freed it as I got close enough to the shimmering air, swinging it upwards. Blue sparks scattered in all directions, decimating his barrier. My other hand was already reaching for the taser. I wasn't going to have time to tie this one up. I squeezed the trigger as the magically enhanced spines flew from the gun taking their shock-inducing charge with them. The enforcer fell in half speed which would have been funny at any other time.

My head started to hurt. Pushing through the slowed down time like this took its toll. I let go and the man crashed to the ground at normal speed. I didn't have time to study the box, someone was bound to look round any second. I hefted the escrima stick and brought it down on the door lock with all my might, hoping it would be enough to bring down any defences or wards the box may have. The door caved in straight away and I launched in, pulling it to behind me.

Spinning round, I opened my mouth to call Baxendale's name but I froze. I was in the middle of a box, no bigger than ten-foot square and yet I was staring at a front room, complete with tv, sofa...and a window. A staircase to a balcony bedroom was off to the left. All in all it would have made a lovely holiday home. It definitely did not look like a ten-foot prison cell.

"Hello?" A man appeared round a dividing wall, a glass in his hand. He looked terrified at my appearance.

"Hi. Are you Lee?" I narrowed my eyes.

"Umm, yeah. How did you get in? Who are you?" He stepped backwards, eyes darting round to look for some kind of defence. I'm not ashamed to admit, I stared open-mouthed for a few seconds. The man was in a magical construct and he had no idea he was even a prisoner. Well this would be fun.

"Right, ok. My name's Remi." I marched over to the man who was now cowering against a fridge. How could this guy be important and dangerous enough for all this? I grasped his arm. "Believe it or not, but I'm a friend and your best option is to just come with me and don't ask questions until we get out. Alright?" He tried to wiggle out of my grasp but he didn't stand a chance. The man was about four inches shorter and barely filled out his woollen jumper. "Look. I'm here to break you out."

"Of my house?" He started pulling even harder.

"Just look out the door a sec." I hauled him across the room and pulled open the door, propelling him into the gap. He let out a squeal before leaping back in.

"What the..?"

"Exactly. Those mean looking lot out there, they're going to hurt us." The colour drained out of his face. "So, do exactly what I say, when I say alright?"

"Who are they? Where am I?" His eyes were wide enough to look painful. The guy honestly had no clue. Someone had gone to a lot of trouble to keep him happy in his box. This really was starting to feel wrong. I heard a shout and footsteps headed our way.

"So much for distraction." I leaned my head out of the door, feeling a tingle I hadn't noticed as I entered. One of the men from the table had spotted his compadre on the floor and was closing in. I stepped out of the door, motioning for Lee to stay back and readied myself but the man had disappeared. I heard the air moving above me before I realised. Damned shifters. I darted to my left as the gravitational mage dropped from the air with a thud. The clamour had attracted the attention of the woman who'd been sitting with him. I did a quick sweep of the floor but couldn't spot the others. I pulled the taser out of the holster and tried to get an aim on the shifter who was as good as flying in the air above me. Just as I had him, a blast of air knocked into my hands with the force of a bulldozer. My fingers loosened their grip instantly and the weapon clattered to the floor, only to be carried further away by another directed gust from the woman.

"He had to say good luck didn't he." The shifter swooped down at me again so I grabbed my escrima and swung at his legs, knocking him off balance and bringing him down to the floor. I closed my eyes and willed time to slow, allowing me to close in on the woman. The best weapon I had was knowing the limitations of all the different types of mages. A fire mage couldn't do too much if you kept them cold enough, opposite was true for an ice mage. A psychic mage could be bombarded with too many thoughts. The woman in front of me was a displacement mage, or as I liked to call them, windy mages. The council didn't half like to give complicated fancy names. To build up enough energy in the air she was displacing, she needed to be far away. Get up close and she couldn't build up enough strength to do much more than tickle. I used my control over the speed of time to close the gap and let go as I sent my elbow to her face.

A familiar clicking noise drew my attention as she punched back and connected on my jaw. As I spun on my heel, I caught sight of two enforcers with guns trained on me. One was leaning out from behind the kitchen door and another was on the stairs in the middle of the warehouse. They hadn't been there before. I rolled across the floor, out of the way of the woman's foot and spotted two more enforcers re-entering the warehouse from the front entrance.

I felt air shifting above me as the shifter started a downward descent. I concentrated, caught hold of the moment and used the stretched seconds to propel me back into the box with Lee. I threw my weight against the door and sat against it, hoping whatever wards were on this thing meant they couldn't get in or shoot through.

"Guns. They have guns," I hissed. "We don't use projectiles on other mages. It's just, just not how we do things."

"Guns? They're going to shoot us?" I ignored Lee's sobs of terror. The Council would never sanction the use of mundane firearms. Victor was right, there was a new element in play and it would be bad if they got control of the Council, assuming they didn't already have it.

"Ok Lee, I'll admit, not looking good. There are six just in here we have to get through. Two have guns, one can fly, one can throw a tornado at us and I have no idea what the other two have."

"What are you talking about?"

"If I try and take on any of the ones out there, they're just going to shoot me. There's no cover, and no other way out." Lee started muttering but I wasn't really listening to him. Or talking to him really, I just needed to hear it out loud. "I can move quickly if I slow down the rest of you but not enough. Unless…"

I had tried this once before and I'd slept for two days straight afterwards. My power worked in small bursts, affecting the area close to me. I slowed everything around me down and I pushed through. When I exerted my will on another object with a lot of force, for example, punching them, everything sped up. But if I could affect a larger area? I tried to ignore the pounding on the door behind my back. I pushed everything out of my head and remembered the scene in my head that I first conjured up when I was training. A beach, the sunset was casting purple hues across the sky. A moment paused so I could bask in the colour forever. I could feel the sand under my knees and against my feet. It was warm but not too hot. I could smell the salt of the sea but I could hear nothing. Everything was frozen. I wallowed in the stillness, brought it inside of me. I felt the sensation build. When I felt I could take no more, I let the feeling expand, leave me and exert itself on everything around me. As it left, a wave of exhaustion hit but I rocked with it, allowing it to pull at me but not rip my concentration away. I held the image of the beach in my mind as I opened my eyes. Lee was stuck in a moment of babbling fear, staring at me. The pounding on the door had stopped.

I stood up and opened the door. Tornado woman had moved back and her hands were ready to fire at the door. I moved slowly and carefully towards her. I took a deep breath and gripped her arms, edging her round, feeling the exertion pull at my will but not allowing it to overwhelm my control. She spun on the spot as I aimed her at her colleague coming in from the opposite door. Next, I moved as fast as I dared towards the gunmen. All I had to do was shut the door to the kitchen to impede the first man. The second took a little more effort as I pulled him towards the edge of the stair. When time restarted, he would overbalance and fall down the stairs.

My eyes were starting to feel fuzzy, pressure was building up in my head. I took a deep breath and made my way to the door. The sight started to make me feel ill. I had drastically underestimated the number of enforcers. Where had they all come from? There were more like twenty-five of them crawling over the ground outside. Flames were paused in mid dance over the building opposite. Not the most subtle distraction, yet effective. I moved as quickly as I could back to Lee, not daring to break into a run as it would break my hold. As I got closer to the box, I spotted my taser and scooped it up. I slid back behind the door but craned out around it, aiming my taser at the shifter. I let go of my hold and fired instantly, the pins of the shot hitting him squarely in the chest. He jerked violently before dropping to the floor like a sack of stones on top of his friend who had just sent the man at the end of the room flying. The sounds of men falling and shots hitting doors flooded my senses. The stillness being replaced with sudden violent noise threatened to overwhelm me. I waved Lee closer and he crawled around the sofa on his hands and knees.

"Helios," I muttered, my voice showing the strain. "I'm on the ground floor but the enforcers outside will on top of us in a few seconds."

"What's that?" Lee was pulling on my shirt, pointing furiously at the back wall. I was about to bat him away when I saw what he meant. The wall was beginning to shimmer, faze in and out of existence in a neat circle. Instinct kicked in and I hauled myself in front of Lee, raising my taser in defence.

The fading circle, completely disappeared, leaving a perfectly round hole in the wall. A head peered through, dark hair dropping over her eyes as she waved frantically at me. "Hurry up!" I grabbed Lee and propelled him towards Victor and the hole. As I got closer, I saw there was a corresponding hole in the outer wall of the warehouse.

"Neat," I mumbled as I climbed through the hole.

"What the hell is that?" Victor peered into the void for another second before, resealing it.

"No idea," I shook my head. "But at least it will be a minute before they realise we're not in it." I waved Victor out of the hole in outer wall. She jumped ahead and pushed Lee into my car that was waiting.

Helios was standing beside the vehicle poised and ready. "Castigan?"

"Not this time," I replied grimly as I fell into the open door to the back seat. Victor slid into the driver's seat and started the engine. A roar of another fire drowned out the car as gusts of heat blew in. Helios climbed in and the car started moving before he'd even shut the door.

"Lee, this is Helios and Miss Victor. Victor, Helios, this is Lee. We're taking you to see the Queen. Now, talk amongst yourselves for a bit, yeah?" I didn't hear a response before I fell back against the seat, unconscious.


**Alex Minns** is an England-based writer who has worked as a scientist, teacher and has, in the past, been paid to explode custard powder on a regular basis in the name of science. She writes a range of scifi, steampunk and urban paranormal fiction. You will also find her on twitter obsessively creating micro fiction as Lexikonical. Currently, she is working on a steampunk novel with time travel and trying to not get confused!

# World of Your Dreams
## by Chris Bauer

Cliff glared at the emails on his laptop. Another rejection by an agent for his novels.

French doors led to his narrow balcony, one of a string along the second floor of the old 1920'S apartment building. He should be enjoying the weather, two stories above the street. But not now.

"Excuse me."

The voice pulled Cliff from his maelstrom of frustration.

Anna Biggs stood at the balcony divider holding a flash drive. Gentle features, glasses, dark hair framing her face. Always friendly. Always cheerful. She struck Cliff as not knowing she was beautiful. He would have tried to be more than neighbors but right now the damned novels—no, more accurately the process of finding an agent—pushed him to the edge of mental exhaustion. Being published meant he was who he believe he was...and proved Jane wrong.

Success. The sweetest revenge.

"May I borrow your printer? Mine is going crazy. I'll bring my own paper," said Anna.

"You don't have to bring your own paper."

She climbed over the railing with her tote bag. The laptop's screen saver showed Cliff and a blonde beauty with a starlet's figure, their arms around each other's waist.

"Wow," said Anna. "She's beautiful."

"My Ex." He didn't even have time to change the screen saver to the mass- produced innocuous nature scene.

"Oh." She looked like she wanted to say more but stopped short

"Here," said Cliff. "Go ahead. You drive."

She didn't take his chair but crouched, inserted the flash drive, opened the file, and pressed print. A soft whir and the whoosh of paper came through the open doors.

They went in together, and she took a dozen pages of what looked like a library catalog. "Thank you." She slipped the papers into her bag. "You're a writer, aren't you?"

"A writer with a real job." He laughed. "All I can sell are short stories. I'm in the top tier of the second tier."

"Novels are hard to sell," said Anna. "The same millionaire authors over and over again. Then they have other people write their books for them."

"You're right," said Cliff. "Something's wrong with this world."

Anna dropped her papers into the tote, rummaged through it, and extracted a book. "I know this will help. You can get published. You can get almost anything, within reason."

Cliff took the book, trying to be polite. "*Create the World of Your Dreams?*"

"It's about cognitive dreaming. You have to actualize your dream before somebody does it for you."

He read the back cover. "Multiple parallel dream realities."

"Yeah. It sounds weird but it works." She put her hand on his arm. "Read it. Please."

Cliff had done everything else to get published...and to forget about Jane gloating at his failure. He sensed Anna watching him with inexplicable expectation. "OK. I will."

"Well, uh, thanks for letting me use your printer," she said, and climbed over the railing.

Cliff brought in his laptop. He had enough rejection for one day. He set the laptop on his old wooden filing cabinet stuffed with unpublished novels and published short stories.

He touched a key, and the laptop returned to his email

'Your novel *Flying Monkeys* is unsuitable for our needs at this time.' Cliff opened the next message.. 'Due to the death of our associate John Carter, your submission *Law of Equivalence*—'.

"We have a winner for the Creative Rejection Award!" Cliff announced.

He went to the kitchen cabinet and pulled out a bottle of bourbon. Cliff ignored the glasses and took a swig directly from the bottle.

He came back to see his screen saver. "You were right, Jane. I didn't fit in with your friends." Cliff opened the filing cabinet and pulled out a 1920's Remington pocket pistol, then refiled the gun under 'G'. "I don't need this. I have nothing to steal," he said to the empty room. He picked up the bourbon bottle and took another drink.

Cliff left Jane, so maybe this was her revenge.

A slip of paper poked from the book Anna gave him. A phone number, and the words 'We could talk over coffee some time."

"I'm a mess. Why do you want to know me?" Nobody answered.

Cliff selected a collection of Kafka stories from a mini-bookshelf and went to his bedroom.

God, he hoped he slept well tonight.

\*     \*     \*

Live, 1920's music came from the next room.

He sprawled on a plush leather sofa, in a large room with a large, open liquor cabinet. The wide windows showed the darkness of night, with faint streetlights blurred by tress. An Art

Deco desk with a Courier manual typewriter and desk lamp faced a new wooden filing cabinet.

He picked up a glass of ice and whiskey from the end table and took a long sip.

He didn't belong here.

Jane swished in, wearing a skin-tight white sequin dress, holding a cigarette holder in one hand and a drink in the other. The long strand of pearls hanging from her neck shimmered in the light. "People are asking for you."

"Your people or my people?" His words slurred. "I forgot. I don't have any people."

"I wouldn't dream of making you successful" Cliff remembered she was good with sarcasm.

"I got by on my own," said Cliff.

Jane thrust the cigarette holder at him like a dagger. A curl of hair slid out of place onto her forehead. "I'm not letting you throw away everything we worked for."

"It's like a bad dream."

Jane shook her head and smiled like a tigress. "You'll never figure it out."

"Figure out what?" said Cliff.

Jane took a deep breath, stood up straight, brushed the curl back in place, and strode through the door. "Scott! Zelda! It's so good to see you."

Cliff pushed himself off the sofa, and for a moment, wobbled. Too much to drink. He took a swallow from the glass anyway. And with only one misstep made his way to the filing cabinet. "Under G," he said to himself. He pulled open the drawer and brought out a new, Remington pocket pistol. Cliff stumbled back to the sofa, laid the pistol beside the glass, closed his eyes and rubbed his temples.

"Mr. Brown!" said Anna.

He opened his eyes to see her standing in a maid's outfit and apron, a serving tray in hand. "Please don't."

"Don't what?"

"People like your stories. You're in all the big magazines. People buy them just for your stories." A pleading tone touched her voice.

Cliff shook his head. "I wanted to write amazing things that…" He lost the thought.

Anna stepped closer, and knelt to be eye level with him. "You do."

"I take crap and make it Hollywood screenplay crap."

Anna slid the pistol from the end table into her apron pocket.

Cliff squeezed his eyes shut. If only he could make this world go away.

He heard each click as Anna stripped the bullets from the pistol magazine. He opened his eyes to see her standing in the doorway with the bullets in her apron pocket and tray in hand. For a moment, Anna looked back at him, hesitating in the doorway.

"Do I know you?" he asked.

"You're supposed to. Please read the book."

Cliff sank into the sofa and squeezed his eyes shut. The numbing of the whiskey finally took effect, and he could feel himself slipping into sleep.

*    *    *

He drove like he knew the streets, out of instinct. The rational part of his brain marveled at how he could drive to a place he had never been. He turned at a familiar street sign—one he had never seen before—SEASIDE BOULEVARD.

Anna stood outside of Literal Lovers, purse over her shoulder, an ID card hanging on a lanyard around her neck. The dark windows of the bookstore reflected the sunshine of the street, and a couple employees stood on the sidewalk, reading. Cliff pulled into the parking place marked with orange cones. "What happened?"

"The power shut off. They said something overloaded and won't be fixed in time." Her eyes went wide. "Are you Cliff Brown?"

He considered whether he was or wasn't, then decided he was. "Yes."

She grabbed his hand. "It is so cool to meet you! I mean, after *'Repetitive Stupidity Disorder'* you write *'Flying Monkeys'* and then you come right out with *'Law of Equivalence'*, and it's funny but serious…"

"It's good to meet you." Cliff spoke the words not from practice, but out of sincerity. She was familiar, the only constancy in the last couple…days? "I guess there's no book signing today?"

"I'm so sorry. We'll have to postpone. Can I buy you a cup of coffee? For…the inconvenience, I mean. You can tell me about how you write."

"Sorry. I have to get going." A mandatory task called him back to the house. Something dark and violent lingered in his mind, and he left it unchallenged.

Cliff cruised into the driveway with the car in neutral, the engine a deep throated purr rather than a roar. He unlocked the front door and paused to listen. From rooms away, he heard the distinctive sounds of love-making; a squeaking bed, a man's sensual growl, and a woman's voice—Jane's voice—moaning with pleasure. Cliff knew where the gun was—in the file cabinet, under 'G'.

He slipped out the magazine to find the gun unloaded. A vague memory of bullets in an apron pocket came to mind, but he had no time to puzzle it out. Cliff pulled out desk drawers one after another until he found the box of cartridges. He loaded the magazine and snapped it into the pistol and took a deep breath. He crept toward the bedroom, the plush carpet swallowing his footsteps. Cliff hesitated outside the door.

Jane straddled Carter, grinding her hips, eyes closed and gasping with each thrust.

"A hell of an agent you are," said Cliff.

John Carter turned his head. He bolted upright, throwing Jane onto the bed.

"Cliff, this isn't what—"

"It's not?" Cliff smiled and shrugged. "OK." He turned to leave. Spinning, he pointed the gun and pulled the trigger. Carter fell back on the bed, the hole in his chest spewing blood. Jane turned. God, she was so beautiful. Even when stabbing him in the back. Cliff shot her. Once. In the heart, or where she should have one. She fell back onto Carter. "Now you're really together." Cliff didn't like the cruel tone in his voice. He felt detached and nauseous at the same time, as if writing a bad screenplay. Carter's hand lay on Jane's face.

"Get your hands off her you girl-friend-stealing son of a bitch." Reaching down, he flung the bloody hand aside.

Cliff stumbled into the hallway, leaning back against the wall. He shut his eyes and slid down until he sat on the floor. An emotion kept punching him in the stomach. Regret? No.

Confusion.


*       *       *

Banging on his apartment door.

Almost noon. Saturday. Anna's book lay open on his lap, not the Kafka stories. Cliff rubbed his eyes. God, what a nightmare. The bourbon bottle on the bed stand held only one swallow. No wonder the bad dreams.

The banging on the door stopped.

Cliff dressed, made a cup of coffee, and went onto the balcony for fresh air.

Anna waited. "I got published!" She waved the magazine. "I knew it would work!"

"Congratulations." Cliff expected to find only the usual rejections in his email.

Anna brought the book from behind her back. She spoke with urgency. "Now, you have to promise you'll read this today. Before you go to sleep. Please."

Cliff studied the book, "*Creating the World of Your Dreams.*" He was certain it was the book he left on his bed. He turned it over and read the back flap. "I read some of this last night." He remembered taking the book with him and waking with it. "How did you get this?"

"It's my copy."

She radiated a contagious cheerful enthusiasm. Cliff could only smile. "I've been having these nightmares…" Babbling. A sure way to impress her, he thought. He gripped the book like a man on a sinking ship would a life preserver. "I'll start right now." Cliff went into the kitchen for some coffee and breakfast bars.

"Please read it before it's too late," Anna called after him.

\*     \*     \*

Cliff had dozed off. Too much of the celebration party last night. He stretched out in the lounge chair, the Pacific Ocean breeze fluttering the white gauze curtains. The air smelled like California. He remembered the book, and found it on the floor beside him, dog-eared and the cover worn. He reread part of it every day.

Anna came through the French curtains in an explosion of white. She wore a tennis dress, and glowed luminous. *"New York* magazine wants a review and a poem from me every issue!"

Cliff climbed from the lounge chair, wrapped his arms around her, and pulled her next to him. "I knew you'd get it. You're marvelous."

"Not as marvelous as Mister Best-Selling-Two-Books-of-Collected-Stories-In-Nineteen-Twenty-Five," she said, and kissed him; a long, loving, passionate kiss. Holding hands they walked out to the patio, the trees throwing shade over the table with his typewriter.

"You wouldn't believe the dreams I had," said Cliff. "Material for a couple short stories."

Jane, in her maid's uniform, and wearing a blank expression, set the table for breakfast. Cliff didn't remember hiring her. Jane left with the empty tray, picked up the book, and went through the bedroom doors rather than into the kitchen.

"She has the book!" Cliff leapt from the table after her.

Like his favorite author, **Chris Bauer** started writing as an unemployed oil company manager. Since then, he has acquired 35 (now 36, thanks to Cloaked Press) paid fiction publishing credits. The short stories include killer squirrels, flying monkeys, demons disguised as cats and a 'true' story about a WWII fighter pilot related by Chris's father. He's currently working on an alternative history/steampunk novel set in 1854---what if Napoleon hadn't sold Louisiana to the US in 1803?

## Stardust & Lies
## by Mato J. Steger

Rain sliced at Jeff's face like sharp pins. His chest heaved as puddles soaked into his old sneakers. That greasy bastard had Lily, and for what? Some *stardust* batch gone wrong? Jeff had followed orders, picked up and delivered the package. That was it. Leave it to a junky to think a twelve-year-old kid would steal his drugs.

He hurried as fast as he dared on the slick concrete. Lily was in trouble. *Get to her. Save her.* He had just shown up to the school when Balthazar slipped the sack over her head and tied her up. Jeff had snuck through the shadows and peaked around the corner as Lily thudded into the trunk of the beat-up sedan.

*Damn it. If Leroy was still alive…*

No. That kind of thinking didn't help. He couldn't bring back the dead, not that Leroy could have helped in his condition anyway. The man had starved to death in a cold tent, all so Jeff could survive. Leroy had given him too much already.

The graffiti down Elm Street marked a No Man's Land. He ducked around a corner and watched the back of one the gang members he'd tailed drop into a moss-covered manhole, leaving the cover askew.

"What's the plan, boss?" Rex hissed out from his place curled under Jeff's hood. The squeaky little dragon came around six months ago. At first Jeff thought his magic had wished the dragon into life. Rex had been a teddy bear found in his dimly lit apartment. The same

118

apartment Mr. CEO rented for Jeff in exchange for his continued work transporting *stardust*. The moonlight struck through the bedroom window, and what had once been Rex the teddy bear slithered and twisted in a puff of fluffy cotton spreading out in a confetti across the room. It opened like an egg, as if the dragon had been inside the whole time. *What's up, Jeff?* Had been Rex's first words. Jeff promptly peed himself. It took a while to realize Rex wasn't imaginary, though Lily thought he was some foreign lizard with a name Jeff couldn't pronounce.

Jeff halted. "I don't know. Save Lily." He flattened himself against an art-colored wall of a Dia de Los Muertos woman with flowers in her hair. The halo of her Sacred Heart's flame burned above his head. Seconds dripped by as rain soaked through his cotton hood. The manhole cover didn't so much as shake. A few more seconds, and it'd be safe to slip in.

The cross at his neck itched, and he slammed his hand against it. *"Lord of the Powers be with us, for in times of distress we have no other help but You. Lord of the Powers, have mercy on us."* Jeff muttered the prayer three times.

He remembered the prayers and saints of his childhood. Before his parents left him at age six in Dallas without even a good-bye. Before Leroy scooped him off the sidewalk and raised him, taught him as much as he could. The prayers never left him, he needed his Saints now more than ever.

Still no movement.

Jeff pushed off the wall, clasped the lip of the manhole cover and dragged it back. It grated across the concrete. He squinted his eyes, looking both ways. Still clear. His chest strained, arms beginning to ache.

*Why is this thing so heavy?* He grumbled, shoving as hard as he could.

A bit of gratitude rose in him that the *stardust* he lugged around for Mr. CEO helped him build muscle. Even if it was this stupid job's fault Lily was in this mess. *That I'm in this mess!*

"What's that smell? Sewer?" Rex coiled and fluttered his wings, swishing Jeff's gray hair back and forth. He always wanted to dye it, but now wasn't the time for vanity.

"Yeah." The dark hollow echoed back at him. Only the dim cracks of light through the Dallas rainy sky highlighted the top of the ladder.

The putrid stench of death and decay burned at his nostrils as he lowered himself into the depths that may as well have been hell. Everyone on the street knew what happened beneath Dallas. Everyone stayed clear of the stars below if they knew what was good for them. And now, because of his lies, Lily might die down there. A world she shouldn't even know existed. A world of secrets worse than his own. He had to save her.

The metal squeaked as his shoes caught purchase on each invisible rail. Rex held tight to his neck, his scales a comforting scratch as Jeff reached up and slid the manhole shut, plunging them into darkness.

A girl's scream reverberated through the tunnel.

"Lily." Jeff's voice cracked the way she loved to tease him about. "I'm coming... I'm coming, just hold on."

The rush of water grew louder as he descended, until his foot hit solid ground.

"Flame or lantern?" He asked Rex. For a silly, little dragon, Jeff would be still doing useless parlor tricks without his guidance. Leave it to a dragon to know how warlock magic worked.

"Lantern, I can smell the methane from here. Let's not get charred to pieces."

Jeff took a deep breath, trying not to gag. He placed both hands at his sides, palms open, facing up. With all his might, he thought of happiness. Lily's smile. The way her eyes lit when he mastered history. The way she laughed when he put the emphasis in the wrong part of a new word. The way she hugged him tight like she never knew when she might see him next.

Light poured from his fingertips. He circled his hands, forming an orb of light and raising it just above his head. This was a trick he had done for people in the park, but whenever they asked how, he just smiled and said, *"A magician never reveals his secrets."* In truth, he had no idea how he did it, just that he could.

Blessed by the Saints, he was sure, though a part of him feared it wasn't a blessing if his parents didn't see fit to keep him. It wasn't until he was older he realized the divide between those who were *unique* and those who weren't. Whatever the reason his parents left him, it was Leroy's smarts that kept him safe, helped him get his spot in the park as a street performer.

The concrete tunnel illuminated. Relief flowed out with his next breath. The corridor remained empty, save the rushing river of yuck. Keeping to the edge, he moved the direction he thought the scream had come from. The farther he moved, the smaller the gap of darkness became. A short distance away, artificial light poured out from a small corridor off the other side of Yuck River.

"How do I cross?" He whispered to Rex.

"You and I both know how you cross." Rex tipped his beakish nose against Jeff's collarbone. "Think of it like training, sometimes we do things the hard way for the best results."

"No. Absolutely not, that's… gross." Jeff curled his lip. He hated when Rex spoke truths. Even though for months now that's all the little dragon had ever done.

"Hey, it isn't my fault you don't have wings."

"Carry me across." Jeff felt like begging.

"You're too big. Get swimming. You do know how to swim, don't ya?"

"Shut up." Of course, he could swim. Leroy made sure he knew the basics. But, swim… in that?

"Get off me!" Lily's shouts echoed through the sewer.

"Dammit!" Jeff dropped into the murky water.

The current tugged at his jeans. His feet met the bottom and gripped concrete. The green muck reached to his chest. Why couldn't he be taller? He scrunched his nose. Shoving himself forward, he focused on Lily's hazel eyes, vibrant in their shine, but dark with mystery.

Gurgling and hacking noises bounced off the walls causing his chest to tighten.

He swam faster. Reaching the other side, he gripped the ledge and pulled himself up.

Rex's claws dug into his neck. "Someone's coming."

He let the orb vanish, plunging them back into darkness. The trickle of illumination down the corridor focused into a flashlight. It moved closer.

Soaked in murky waste, Jeff felt for the wall and crouched down. The light arched closer, but it was too bright to see beyond it. A lump rose in his throat. Steps thumped closer.

The light vanished. He heard someone breathing. Ice chilled his veins.

He had never been in a real fight. A few scuffles with kids on the street, who bullied him because he looked different. But being different didn't mean he couldn't protect himself. Rex kneaded his shoulder and Jeff clenched his fists.

A boot touched his thigh. Before he could lunge, a hand grabbed the collar of his hoodie and yanked him up.

"Who are you?" The girl's voice demanded. "Don't think you're going to get the chance to tie me up again." She shoved him against the algae-covered wall.

Rex groaned.

Jeff knew that voice. "Lily?"

The flashlight flicked back on. Hazel eyes met his.

"Jeff? What are you doing down here? Do you *know* those men?"

"I-I-I…" *I what? I work with them? Sort of… I lied to you when I said I live with my parents near North Park?*

"You what?" Her eyes widened. She released him. The light went off. "Shh… They're coming."

This had been his rescue mission, and yet, here he was soaked in yuck, hiding like a coward in the dark.

Boots clunked. Lights came on down the tunnel. Jeff bit the inside of his cheek wishing he could summon a cloak of shadows to disguise them and damned himself for only knowing light tricks and minor illusions.

"Where the hell is she?" A man shouted. Balthazar. He could hear the ugly rasp of a man who drank too much whiskey in his voice. "What did you do? Did you let her go?"

"No, she… She knocked me out!" The second man's voice heaved and rasped. Jeff couldn't tell who it was, but he understood the sputtering of one of Balthazar's henchmen, dubbed *"The Stars"*. *Godless gang of bastards.*

"You let some little girl knock you out? Get the hell up, you, pathetic wretch!"

"What did you do to him?" Jeff whispered, righting himself. Lily stood a few inches from him, heat radiating off her.

"I used the useless ropes he tied around my wrists to strangle him. Kind of glad, he didn't die. I'm too young to be a murderer," she

125

said with a shrug, off-handedly, but true to her as anything else might be.

"Wouldn't any age be too young to be that?"

"In Dallas?" She snorted. "You're really sweet, Jeffy, but you can't be that naïve. Now, help me do this before they figure out where we are."

"Do what?"

"My plan. Those men are going to regret kidnapping me. Hope they can swim."

Lily nudged him to the side and he could hear her light rattling in her other hand.

"I saw a lever when they brought me down here. All you need to do is swim across and yank it down to open the floodgate."

Jeff groaned. "I just went through that. Isn't there another way up?"

She grabbed his arm. "I have a sneaking feeling you know these scumbags, somehow. I'm also pretty sure you don't go to Westford Junior High. Considering ... no one's heard of you. So, see this as retribution for me. Compensation on your part. Like my dad always says, when you borrow something, you must pay it back. You borrowed my trust. Now it's time to pay me back."

"I… How did you find out?" Jeff furrowed his brow, gaze darting back down the tunnel. "When did you find out?"

"Does that matter right now? Long enough, I just figured you'd tell me, Jeffy. Eventually anyway, before high school, maybe? We don't have time to talk about this right now." He could feel her eyes digging into him, even if it was too dark to tell.

Jeff bit his tongue. "Can you turn the light back on then?"

"That's part of the plan. I set the light, we cross the water, you hit the lever. Just follow orders, and everything will be fine." She squeezed his shoulder. "Everything will be fine." Her voice soothed his mind.

"Okay."

The light in the distance danced in and out of view as the men's shadows came out into the corridor. Forcing himself across, Jeff crawled back up the other side, dripping and waiting for the light. The light clicked on. For a half-second Jeff saw Lily's face, her eyes dark and brow furrowed, blood dried on her cheek. Was it her blood? Or the strangled man's?

She swam faster than him. Before he could get to the lever she was at his side.

"Ready? You hit the lever, then we both go up the ladder."

"Yeah." He wished he could see better. His gut twisted in on itself, pulling this lever wasn't penance enough for the years of lying. It wasn't. He could tell the Father a hundred times his sins, but he couldn't risk being taken by the state as their ward.

"Hey! Come back here, you little bastards!" Balthazar shouted and grabbed the lantern where Lily had left it, lowering himself into the river, his partner just behind.

"Now, Jeff!"

He pulled the lever and heard the metal gate open. A rush of water burst out. Jeff followed Lily down the small concrete path and gripped the bottom of the ladder as she climbed. The water crashed into Jeff's side, his jeans pulled, and one of his sneakers yanked off into the dark waters.

Screams echoed along the tunnel, then became muffled by gurgles. Jeff squeezed his hands tight to the bars. If Balthazar saw him, recognized him… If he lived… *It may be time to start looking for a new job... and life.*

Lily opened the manhole and yanked him up, a wry smile on her face. "Now, how are you going to make all this adventuring up to me? I was thinking… Oh, I don't know… ice cream. And you tell me everything. All of it. The truth."

"Think we can get a change of clothing first?" He let out a laugh.

Lily rolled her eyes. "Only so I don't regret being seen like this."

He nodded, the sun cracking through the rain clouds. Ice cream and telling her everything was a good start, but he was certain he would happily spend the rest of his life making it up to her if she let him. Rex nuzzled his neck. Jeff was certain if anything, the little dragon couldn't agree more.

**Mato J. Steger** is a Fantasy and Scifi writer who dabbles in horror and the occasional contemporary romance. His work has been featured with two short stories in an anthology called Infinite Darkness in 2017, as well as several of his articles have been featured in Queer Voices for the Huffington Post. He writes for The Ascent, a motivational ezine on Medium, while living with his partner in the United States. He currently holds a Bachelor's Degree in English & Creative Writing from Southern New Hampshire University.

# Museum of Lost Souls
## by David Cleden

Madam Celeste, Head Curator at the Museum of Lost Souls, cleared her throat and drew the group's attention back to the large sign which read 'Strictly No Visitors.'

Possibly she was expecting a titter or a polite smile but the group of initiates gave her nothing except a puzzled silence.

Her gaze swept over the new intake. "You must not underestimate the importance of our job," she told them. "We are both custodians _and_ restorers. It goes without saying that the Museum's Exhibits are unique and irreplaceable. And--" she gave a theatrical sigh, "the sad truth is the Collection grows larger by the day."

She gestured behind her and the group obediently raised their gaze to the splendid hall which seemed to stretch onwards until the details became lost to darkness and perspective.

This is too much, Kadia thought. I shouldn't even be here.

Others in the group shuffled uneasily. High above them, fluted marble columns met and intertwined with snakelike grace. Every fifty feet or so were side galleries, left and right: narrow, high-walled chambers, their doors chained open. (All except one, Kadia noted, whose heavy wooden door was firmly closed). Within each gallery, the walls were lined with shelves upon which the Exhibits were displayed. Superficially, each was similar: a glass-stoppered bell jar, twelve inches tall. In the Museum's dim light (which barely rose above perpetual gloom) their dusty surfaces shimmered with reflections that hid their contents.

What took Kadia's breath away was the sheer scale of the place. It seemed possible--if understandably impractical--for the halls and galleries to simply continue forever.

How am I supposed to know what to do? Kadia wondered. Do they give us some kind of map?

Madam Celeste's gaze alighted on Kadia. "I cannot teach you how to do your job. That is something you must find out for yourself. And you will--all of you--in time."

She walked a few paces into the nearest gallery, waiting patiently while everyone shuffled in behind. Then Madam Celeste lifted a bell-jar from the shelf, chosen at random from among many hundreds in this side gallery, cradling it with both hands so that it could not slip from her grasp. Its glass was thick and dusty but inside a pale mist stirred, like the swirl of fog across a field on a cold autumn morning. The group craned their necks to catch a better glimpse.

"Each Exhibit deserves your respect. Remember that! Treat the Exhibits with reverence."

She never calls them souls, Kadia thought. 'Exhibits' seemed like such an affectation.

Curious now, Kadia brushed dust from the curved surfaces of a nearby bell-jar. The mist stirred within, fluid and wraith-like. When her fingers made contact with the glass, Kadia felt something flow up her arm and deep inside her mind.

--Oh, my poor boy! My darling! Why was he taken? Oh how my heart bleeds for him. My poor--

Kadia snatched her hand away and the voice died in her head. Yet a sense of loss and despair lingered in her mind, slow to clear.

The bell-jar next to it looked as if it had been there even longer, undisturbed. The glass was darker, almost as if it had once been blackened by fire. The label beneath said: K. MANDL. She let her fingers brush across it--

--In somnis veritas, my friend. Ha! The lies we tell! The lies we tell!

Kadia could sense the dissonance immediately. Here was a soul driven to the edge of madness; forever tortured by the fundamental mismatch between rational mind and maddened soul which could not be reconciled. She sensed in its wild, rambling thoughts that this soul no more belonged with its corporeal body than a left shoe would fit a right foot.

That such a thing could happen surprised Kadia. But then again, why not? Was it any different to people who felt at odds with their sexuality assigned at birth, who, as they grew and developed, came to understand a different truth about themselves? If gender was about more than mere physical categorisation, why couldn't a soul outgrow its corporeal host?

What is it you want? she asked.

The soul of K Mandl seemed to twist and jerk, like some rusted mechanism grinding back into motion. She was getting a clear sense of the soul now; its long isolation had turned it into a corrupt, malformed thing. As the decades had passed it had grown weak and palsied.

--Dream of existence without constraints! Dream of love without limits! Dream of life, life, life! Do you dare to dream, too?

Kadia could feel a potent power, coiled tight like a spring. Mandl's thoughts came to her strongly, as if there was some kind of special bond between them.

Yes, she told Mandl. Sometimes I do.

--Then will you listen to my story? Will you let me show you my truths? Will you let me share myself with you?

The note of desperation brought to mind traps for the unwary. Um. Perhaps not. Sorry.

Please! Let me show you! LET ME SHOW YOU--

Kadia jerked her hand away.

Madam Celeste sounded peeved. "DO NOT touch the Exhibits until you are ready to undertake proper restoration work."

There were titters from the group but Kadia kept her eyes lowered, feeling her face grow hot.

The tour continued, but it was just details. Dull as-- She tried to think of the dullest thing she could remember but gave up. That was the trouble in here, it was so hard to think straight.

They were shown collections ordered by region and history; by ideological conflict and political oppression; epochs of social deprivation and hardship. None of it held Kadia's interest. After a bit she raised her hand.

"Excuse me. Is there some kind of quota to fill?"

In the silence that followed, everyone turned to stare, but Madam Celeste's gaze was the one that made Kadia's skin prickle. She pressed ahead regardless. "You know--a certain number of restorations to complete? And then we're done?"

And we leave.

Her unspoken thought hung in the air.

Madam Celeste's expression didn't alter. Yet it seemed to Kadia, the woman was a taller and more imposing figure than she had been just a few moments ago.

"Whatever gave you that idea, young lady? There is no quota to be filled," Madam Celeste told her.

#

"You'll be fine," Nico said.

Nico was a rather serious-looking young man. He had a prominent forehead with thick, dark eyebrows and a face that seemed to want to slip naturally into a frown unless directed otherwise. Kadia thought him rather dishy.

"Will I?"

They sat on one of the low sofas in a corner of the Staff Room sipping coffee. The Staff Room was a cavernous space, only made less intimidating by the thick stone columns spaced at regular intervals so that you had to get up and wander around to get a true feel for its dimensions. Flowering vines or some other kind of low-maintenance indoor plant curled up the supporting columns, giving the place an airy, artsy feel. You could get a wide (and surprisingly wholesome) range of hot meals from the long serving bar which never closed and was free to Museum staff. Comfy chairs, sofas, low bookshelves, pool and table-tennis tables were scattered about the space. In a distant corner, someone was strumming a guitar quietly. Several tables in the dining area were currently occupied by foursomes playing card games.

"I mean-- I'm not sure there's a choice, is there?"

"We always have choices." Nico steepled his fingers and gazed at her in a way that Kadia found rather off-putting. "But you want my advice? Take each day as it comes."

Kadia let her gaze travel around the Staff Room. It struck her there was something a little odd about the building's geometry and the arrangement of halls and galleries, but she couldn't put her finger on it.

135

One entered the Staff Room by entrances off the Main Hall or one of the connecting corridors which apparently led to yet more long, galleried halls. Accommodation for Museum staff was directly above, up a twisty stone staircase. Each member of staff had a private room. Kadia's was comfortable enough in a spartan kind of way, although it lacked windows. Whoever designed the Museum had clearly been given no constraints on space but lacked an esthetic sensibility.

"Which zone did you say you worked again?" she asked Nico.

"Third hallway west."

Kadia hadn't explored much. On her first day at the end of her shift, she had ventured down one of the connecting corridors, turning back after walking for what seemed like ages when her nerve failed her. The next hall had been still just a glimmer of light in the distance.

"What's it like working there?"

Nico's frown turned into a grin. "A long walk to work."

#

There was a knack to soul restoration and no one was more surprised than Kadia to find that it came quickly to her. The trick was not to give the souls what they wanted. You didn't give them anything. They had to find it themselves. Her role was to enable that process.

With some Exhibits, it was easy. A suggestion of how to effect a reconciliation; perhaps a fear confronted rather than avoided; a regret that must be learned from and set aside. Often the answer was obvious to Kadia--but not to the soul in question. <u>None so blind as those who own the problem.</u> Or something.

Amongst her early triumphs was the soul of an elderly retiree, a stubborn woman who was spending her few remaining years living in bitterness. As soon as Kadia touched the Exhibit jar she saw the extent of the problem. A decades-long estrangement from her son had left her soul tattered and incomplete. Reconciliation seemed impossible; both parties so deeply entrenched that they'd stopped looking for ways to bridge the gap. But Kadia had sensed a splinter of regret lodged deep in the woman's soul, a memory she herself had suppressed. Working that sliver loose, bringing it back out into daylight took many days, but Kadia persisted, returning again and again to that one gallery.

When finally the deed was done, she saw the speckled mist within the jar thicken and grow brighter. For the merest instant, it seemed to shine as brightly as a sliver of moonlight. By the time Kadia had blinked and her eyes had adjusted, the jar was empty.

She won Employee of the Month five times in a row for the number of Exhibits she restored. Her work cleared many shelves of valuable gallery-space in the process. Kadia would have won for a sixth month had not Madam Celeste presented her with a special <u>I'm a Five-Star Restoration Queen!</u> award which ruled her out of future contention.

If any of her co-restorers resented her aptitude, they never mentioned it, most likely because they knew it counted for nothing. By the time her next shift came round, most of the space Kadia had cleared was already filled by fresh Exhibits. There seemed no end to the supply of lost souls the Museum was willing to accommodate.

Many Exhibits Kadia could do nothing about. Cold cases such as Mandl--the Exhibit she had encountered on her first day--had no obvious path to restoration. Madam Celeste warned her not to try. "Many with vastly more experience than you have not succeeded," she told her.

But of course that only made Kadia all the more determined.

One afternoon, she snuck back into the gallery she had come to know as Main 4-K. According to the sign near the door, it held a small part of the European Conflicts collection (1957-61) although Kadia had done no more than skim read the notice because, well... History. Ughh.

Outwardly, the Mandl exhibit looked no different. From studying it carefully, she thought perhaps the glass might be a little thicker than others; the contents a little murkier. The challenge of it excited her.

She placed both hands on the jar.

A gray mist within began to swirl in rising spirals. Carefully she lifted the jar from the shelf.

--You returned. I recognize your kindred spirit.

I want to help, she told Mandl's soul.

--Why?

Kadia had been wondering that herself. Why not? Isn't that why I'm here?

--I am deemed irretrievably lost and beyond help. You waste your time.

Kadia harrumphed. Oh we all have days like that. Dig deeper. Show me where it really hurts.

--Truly?

The circling mist moved a little faster, becoming a blurred ring of effervescence within its glass prison. It was strangely captivating.

Then, with no warning, the mist collapsed into a tight ball and hurled itself against one side of the jar where Kadia held it--like a cute spaniel one had been petting through the bars of its cage suddenly transformed into a snarling creature thrusting itself against its restraints. Kadia could feel the soul pressing against the glass hard, squirming to find a way to reach her, to get inside her. To become her.

Shocked, the bell-jar slipped from her grasp and shattered on the floor.

Glass shards skittered across the marble tiles. Unrestrained now, the mist spread like spilled milk. Part of it crept over her foot, but in this rapidly dispersing form, the soul's raging power grew weak and timorous.

Somewhere nearby, bells started to clamor.

Footsteps came pounding down the hallway.

The clean-up crew were remarkably efficient. They used hand-operated pumps to vacuum up all traces of the soul from every corner and crevice. These were then carefully deposited back into a replacement jar. They told her Mandl's soul would never quite be complete because tiny fragments were always missed in such circumstances--but then it had hardly been fully intact before.

Kadia was summoned to Madam Celeste.

"I hope you will learn from this unfortunate episode, Kadia."

"I'm very sorry. I never meant--"

"Some of our Exhibits are beyond restoration. All are lost when they arrive at the Museum, but some may be lost forever." Madam Celeste sighed. "I understand that sooner or later all of us are tempted by Exhibits which are beyond our help. One's instinct is to embrace them in order to understand them better. To take them within ourselves, even to make them a part of ourselves, in order to learn what they need." She leaned forward and her expression was severe. "Do not be tempted to do this under any circumstances."

#

Kadia diligently worked the galleries assigned to her. Often, when she had done all that she could with the Exhibits on her work list, instead of returning to the Staff Room she wandered further afield, stepping into silent galleries that looked as if they hadn't been disturbed by staff in a very long time.

She never lingered, perhaps running a finger over a jar or three, stopping to help where the restoration needs were obvious, but always moving on, exploring new galleries.

<u>Searching</u>.

But she couldn't find the one Exhibit she sought. The one she knew had to be <u>somewhere</u>.

Her own.

And what would she do if she found it?

Well. One thing at a time, she supposed. It was so hard to think about the future here. Or the past. Even the present was a challenge. Every time her thoughts turned to making plans or recalling memories, they skittered away like pebbles cast on a frozen lake.

This place. That's what it did to you. It stopped you from questioning things because there was no frame of reference any more.

And that sucked.

#

"Nico? Did you ever try to search for your own soul?"

His hand wavered, spilling a little of the coffee he was pouring. He set the jug back down on the drip tray. "Don't talk about The Job when you're off-duty. You know the rules."

"Oh, come on! What harm is--"

He grabbed her and propelled her by the elbow towards a distant corner of the Staff Room. His voice was low. "I mean it! Better not to think about those kinds of things. It's easier that way."

He started back to retrieve his coffee. "Anyway," he added over his shoulder. "Don't waste your time. You won't find it."

"Why not?"

He sighed. "Because that's not how it works. Trust me."

But she knew he was lying. Whenever anyone said "Trust me" they were always lying.

Nico sighed, as if he could read her thoughts. "Look. How about I show you something else, something really cool, if you promise to drop this. Deal?"

She thought she saw a mischievous look in Nico's eye, so she nodded.

He made her wait until break time was over. When a little bell tinkled indistinctly in the distance, various teams began to drift out for their next shift. Some headed down the connecting corridor for the West-2 and West-3 hallways. Kadia's own group shuffled out into the Main Hall but Kadia and Nico hung back. After a minute or two he drew her down the Main Hall in the opposite direction.

"The closed gallery?" Kadia whispered.

"Uh huh." Nico crouched by the brass door-knob. He touched it in some complicated fashion, but with his body shielding it, she couldn't see what exactly. "Not anymore," he announced, and the heavy door swung open on stiff hinges.

"How did you do that?"

"You learn a few things when you've been here a while."

She looked up into his grinning face. "And how long has that been?"

The grin faded. "Don't ask me that. Don't <u>ever</u> ask me that."

The locked gallery was a great disappointment. Exactly the same as all the others. A narrow, dimly lit place; walls lined with shelves-- except there were fewer Exhibits. And these were varying sizes and shapes. In fact, some were very oddly shaped indeed. At the far end of the gallery was a bell-jar bigger than any she had seen before. It stood taller than Kadia on its low shelf. The label beneath read: CELESTE

She turned to Nico, mouth forming a little 'O' of surprise.

"Now you know," he said. "Did you think Madam Celeste would be any different?"

"But it's so <u>big</u>!"

Nico shrugged. "She's taken more than her share of misfits over the years. That's what comes of getting too caught up in your work. Some souls you just can't help. They don't belong with their corporeal body even if the right key could be found for a restoration. Like your Mandl."

Kadia stared at the outsize jar. Faint mists stirred within, like creatures disturbed from their slumber. She thought she could see dozens of strands: different colors, different textures: some thick and curling like interlocking roots; others as tenuous as wisps of cloud.

"Every now and then Madam Celeste has... re-homed them, I suppose that's the way to think of it. Adopted them into herself. But at a cost." He winked at her. "There's always a cost, isn't there?"

#

--And oh, the dreams! How they tormented her!

She remembered Mandl asking her, <u>Do you dare to dream?</u>

And of course she did, but she also wished that her nights in the Museum could be a formless period of non-being, without memory or event. Instead, strangers flocked to her dreams in their hundreds, like carrion birds to a fresh carcass. People living their empty, soulless lives: mourning the loss of a loved one taken suddenly, or perhaps regretting some missed opportunity or challenge not accepted.

Whatever the reason, their souls had been severed. Some core part of the individuals were lost, their lives diminished. Souls that could not find their way back called out to her for help as they sank deeper into the darkness.

She dreamed she saw the faces of the soulless ones marching against the Museum, hundreds and thousands of them, ghostly pale. Silently screaming out their anguish.

Sometimes she thought she recognized her own face amongst them--and she could not bear the thought.

#

Down the endless winding staircase--

Across a deserted Staff Room--

Down the Main Hall.

The only sound was her bare feet slapping against the cold marble of the floor and her breath coming in ragged gasps. From somewhere came the sound of someone sobbing.

It might even have been her.

She swung at a random bell-jar on a gallery's shelf. The sound of it smashing was harsh amidst the endless hush of the Museum. Shocking, yet so satisfying.

Another fell. And another--glass shards and fragments of soul spilling across the floor. On and on she went. Entire shelves of Exhibits came crashing down, the souls within sparking with little blue flashes of discharge where they rubbed against each other.

Bedlam.

Soon the galleries echoed to the sound of breaking glass and the high keening sound of freed souls.

This! Yes, this is what she wanted! Not the sham of restoration work she had applied herself to. What had any of it achieved? The number of restored souls was insignificant when measured against the vast scale of the Museum; scratch-marks on the wall, not hammer-blows for freedom. And if her work here was futile, damn it to hell and back, but she would destroy the Museum and bring it all to an end!

A tide of souls spilled along the halls, swirling around her feet. Each touch brought an unwanted jolt of longing. Help me! Tell me what to do, what to be, how to redeem myself!

That swelling rank was beyond her help now. There were thousands of them, the number growing all the time. Now as she ran down the Main Hall, she had only to glance left or right into the galleries and the bell-jars tumbled from the shelves. The sound of shattering glass became a roar, a wail, and finally a scream.

Kadia fled, chased by the howling needs of the freed souls, roiling like the silty waters of a river that had burst its banks.

Her breath came in ragged gasps. The enormity of what she had done began to steal over her and her skin was slick with sweat.

Rounding a corner, she found her way blocked by a row of heavy oak doors, their top halves inset with narrow panes of safety glass. Long brass door-handles gleamed from a thousand polishings, unsullied by the touch of human hands.

Kadia knew this place. She had been here once before, on that first day.

The Museum's entrance.

Then she saw them. Dozens--no, <u>hundreds</u>--of faces pressed up against the doors, blocking out all light from beyond. Layers deep, the faces jostled for position as though desperate to catch a glimpse inside. Each was pale and wan: men and women, young and old, all races, colors and creeds. Their eyes were both watchful and yearning.

At Kadia's approach--or perhaps at the sight of the unleashed tide of souls pursuing her--a swirling river that grew deeper and broader by the second--the people outside became agitated. Fists banged against the doors. They cried out their longing and frustration.

They want their souls back, Kadia thought. Lost or otherwise.

She stood in front of the doors, trapped in a rapidly closing vise of her own making.

Then from somewhere above the howling din, she heard something even more terrifying.

Madam Celeste was calling her name.

Not just calling it, <u>screaming</u> it in a manner that implied the world--for her--was about to come crashing down.

Kadia didn't hesitate. She did what she'd known she must do all along. She threw back the bolts and flung open the Museum's doors to the people waiting outside.

A surge of corporeal bodies spilled into the foyer.

Now she was properly caught. If the maelstrom had been bad before, it was much worse now. Souls and corporeal bodies gyrated and bumped. In the melee, Kadia was buffeted and pushed away from the doors, no more able to choose her own path than some tiny soot particle bombarded by Brownian motion.

Yet the most amazing thing was happening. Some of the corporeal bodies and souls were being irresistibly drawn to each other. A lucky few were reuniting--somehow finding each other in that seething mass.

The reunions held no drama. There was no flash of lightning or pop of implosion, just a brief merging like two stereoscopic images fusing to make something with true depth. For an instant, body and soul glowed brighter than the sun, then they were gone. Immediately, the void was filled by the press of new souls flowing into the crowded foyer.

"KADIA!"

Madam Celeste was drawing closer, somehow pushing her way towards Kadia. Her eyes were lit with anger so deep it could have been infinite. "WHAT HAVE YOU DONE?"

Kadia struggled against the push and pull of the crowd, oblivious now to the cries of longing that invaded her mind with each touch. Her progress was slow.

"KADIA!"

Terrified by that shrill cry, she saw Madam Celeste was almost upon her, no more than two or three arms' lengths away. "I'll see that you pay a price for this recklessness!"

Suddenly Kadia understood how Madam Celeste had reached her. Each soul that touched the woman seemed to tremble for a moment. Then it began to fade--and Madam Celeste grew a little broader, a little taller. For an instant, both glowed brighter than before, and then the soul was gone--absorbed into the form of the Museum's Head Curator, now a towering woman-shaped colossus.

She pushed towards Kadia, clearing souls from her path as she came, growing larger and more furious with each absorption.

"Kadia! Look at the damage you're doing to the Museum! Acts of vandalism must be punished! Come here, girl."

Kadia fought against the throng, but the crush of bodies only seemed to close about her, pinning her in place.

"Souls should be free, not kept in a museum!"

"No, Kadia!"

"They'll find their own way back, given time. Did these souls ever really need our help? Did we need to keep them imprisoned in a Museum like some kind of fossilized exhibit?"

Madam Celeste loomed over her; a dark, ominous shadow.

"How little you know!"

She reached down for Kadia with grasping fingers, tiny flickers of green flame sparking across her skin. "They belong to the Museum! Only I decide which Exhibits may be returned!"

Without warning, the press of bodies and souls shifted direction, a random surge that carried Kadia a little deeper into the Museum's hallways. Madam Celeste followed, still towering above her, clearing her way by drawing hapless souls into her like a mother draws its pups close.

And then across that seething sea of desperate faces, Kadia's gaze was drawn to one in particular. Ashen and insubstantial, like all the corporeal forms. A young woman. Just one more lost corporeal body searching for something. But in that woman's expression, she saw a glowing ember of longing and determination refusing to be extinguished.

Kadia recognized herself.

She struggled with renewed effort, pushing forwards towards the figure, who turned now, seeing her clearly.

"Come to me!" Kadia shouted. "Reunite!"

But the face that was her own, regarded her for a moment, then shook her head sadly. We do not fit. We have never belonged together. Why else are you here? The figure turned and became swiftly lost in the crowd.

"Please--!"

The green-flecked hand of Madam Celeste reached down for her. As it did, something touched her leg, tugged at her arm. The tingling contact of yet another soul.

"Join with me," Mandl said. "We have an affinity, you and I. A bond forged from our differences."

The essence of Mandl had begun to solidify. She wondered if his soul would eventually wither and die without the protection of a jar; if they all would. She thought about all the things Mandl had done, the many flaws that pock-marked his soul, none of which he had hidden from her. Had his body lived, perhaps he could have become a changed person. Perhaps.

"Kadia, my soul was never at ease in its body. I sense the same with you. Put your trust in the affinity we share!"

Mandl's spirit nestled against her but it brought no pain of contact. He might still have the strength to force his way inside--but if so, he chose not to.

"KADIA!" Madam Celeste's hand made a grab for her.

There was no time left to decide. She saw that a surprising number of souls were reuniting, more than chance encounter could account for. She supposed that souls, even those not yet properly reconciled, found their way back if they were of a mind to. This chaos she had unleashed was not without some benefit. She herself had always felt herself a misfit. But couldn't strengths and weaknesses be compensated for in the union with another?

She felt Mandl's questioning touch and she gave herself up to it.

Madam Celeste's hand reached her. She felt a moment of burning pain summoning her to the edge of a gaping hole filled with the churning, restless souls of all those Madam Celeste had gathered to her, and Kadia wondered if she had left it too late.

Then the half-forgotten world beyond grew suddenly bright in her vision even as the Museum faded to nothing. We'll find a way to adapt, Mandl whispered in her mind.

The very last thing she saw in that place was a sign, torn from the wall by the press of bodies, now trampled and scuffed on the floor. It read: Strictly No Visitors!

**David Cleden** is a previous winner of the James White, Aeon, and Writers of the Future awards and has had fiction published in Interzone and Metaphorosis amongst other magazines. He's been around long enough to have met Arthur C. Clarke and corresponded with Isaac Asimov, two of his writing heroes.

# When the Last King Dies
## by Jess Ko

"Who is the King?" my sister, Alice, asked. We were out in the woods behind our house, waiting for the bell to ring that would tell us it was time to come inside.

"Dad?"

"No," she shook her head which was adorned a band of twigs tied together with red hair ribbons on top. "I am the King."

She broke a branch off a nearby tree and made me kneel in the dead leaves on the ground. She touched the branch to one of my shoulders and then swooped it over my head to the other. "For your service to the Kingdom of Pines, I knight thee Lady Nora."

"Girls can't be kings," I said.

"Do you want to be a knight or not?"

Of course, I did. "But girls can't be knights either."

"If I am a king, then you are a knight." Her eyes sparkled with fire in the golden dusk light. "Am I your king?" The wind picked up the dead leaves, swirling them around us like a small tornado and I thought it must be a sign.

I bowed my head. "You are my King."

"Then you are my knight." She smiled and lifted the branch from my shoulder. "Rise, Lady Nora, and receive your sword."

I stood. Alice offered me the stick. It was a birch branch, thin and frayed at the end where she broke it off the tree, but when it touched my hand, it transformed into a glittering long sword with garnets inlaid on the hilt. I almost dropped it because it was so heavy in my small hands.

"How did you—"

"Do you swear to serve and protect your King until the end of your days?" The circle of twigs and ribbon in her hair changed too, twisting into a golden crown.

"I swear it."

The bell rang just as the sun dipped below the trees. The sword dissolved in my hands, becoming a simple birch branch again, and Alice's crown turned back into a circlet of twigs and ribbons.

Our childhood days were spent in those woods, protecting our kingdom from the swamp demons that lived in the muck and ferns, fighting the first witch in the battle of the plains, seeking council from the spirits of the moss lands, and drinking the magical sap of the oldest tree in the forest. Alice was a good and just King and I was her most loyal knight, sworn to protect her with my life. Each night after the bell rang, we would place the branch and twig circlet in the crook of large tree where no one but us could find them: my sword and her golden crown, hanging off its hilt.

#

I swear to protect my king until the end of my days," I whispered as I watched the trees slip by the passenger side window as the truck rattled along the abandoned roads, bringing me home for the first time in ten years.

"Did you say something?" The driver, Lewis, asked.

"No, sorry."

The closer we drove toward the center of town, the denser to fog became. I was almost grateful that what would have been the most familiar drive of my childhood was now almost unrecognizable.

"What are you here for, anyway?"

"Collecting some family heirlooms." It was a lie, but an easy one, and the one listed on my application to enter the area. Best to stick to the story.

"That seems like what most folks come back so," he said. "Though there are the crazy ones who come just to gawk or ghost hunt or whatever. They aren't technically allowed but it's not hard to slip through the government's…*rigorous* approval system." I almost laughed, having filled out the single form that got me in here. How much background checking did they do? Probably next to none.

The GPS on the dashboard warned of the driveway up ahead.

"This the one?" Lewis asked.

"Yeah, that's—"

"Shit!" He swerved the car abruptly to the left as a shadow emerged from the trees and bolted across the road in front of us. He hit the brakes and the car jolted to a stop just before the edge of the road. We both slammed into the back of our seats and watched the shadow disappear into the trees beyond us. "Jesus. I'm sorry…that hasn't happened in a while." Lewis put the car in reverse and straightened it out and as he pulled the car back onto the road.

"Goddamn giant bears," he said. "we've been trying to track them for a while now, but they are impossible to catch. I hope it goes without saying that just because the air won't kill you anymore, doesn't mean it's safe here."

"I know," I said.

There could be more blood bears out there, after all.

#

"What are we doing out here, Alice?"

It was late summer and the forest was beginning to darken, the bell would be ringing soon, and we were marching farther into the woods, farther away from home. I clutched the hilt of my sword tightly in my fist, comforted momentarily by its weight which soon, with the sound of the bell, would lift away from me.

"We are going to get my crown back," Alice replied.

"I said we could just make you another one." It was silly that she insisted on going after the crown when it would be simple to get more sticks and string and make a new one.

"It wouldn't be the same," she said somberly, as though some magic would be lost with a replacement. Maybe she was right.

I sighed. "How do you even know where it is?"

"Those crows that took it belong to Yar, the blood bear."

"How do you know that?"

Alice whipped around and I nearly bumped into her. "Because they had blood on their beaks and talons." She wiggled her fingers in front of my face as though her own hands were covered in blood.

"Gross." I took a step back.

Alice looked up at the sky through the arched tree boughs. "We have to hurry, Lady Nora. We don't have much time."

The blood bear, Yar, lived in the moss lands below the cliffs that split the forest into upper and lower halves. We didn't visit the lower forest often. Within it resided the bog, moss lands, and the edge of the river that marked the end of King Alice's domain. It was where the real monsters lived.

We scaled down the cliff faces using strategic rock formations and trees that grew out of the side of the granite as holds. Eventually we reached the bottom. The lower forest felt completely disconnected from the sun-drenched upper areas. This place was damp, cool, and dark from the thick tree cover. The air tasted like the swamp.

"This way." Alice slipped through the tall thin trees with ease and grace. I ran after her, making sure I was always within reach. I had sworn to protect her, after all.

We heard the crows before we saw them. We followed their bleak cries into the moss lands, where the earth was covered in deep green and the trees were sparse and straight, each the same as the one next to it, like columns that rose into the sky, holding the canopy of leaves above our heads like a ceiling.

The giant black bear loomed before us, his clawed paws sinking into the moss, blood pooling into his cavernous footprints. Alice walked toward the beast and stood fearlessly before him, her tiny frame engulfed in his shadow. I wanted to reach out and pull her back, but she knew what she was doing, I had to trust her.

"Will you not bow before your king?" Alice bellowed. The bear stood still, looking down at her. "I've come for my crown."

"Yes, I hoped that you would." The bear's mouth didn't move but his voice echoed across the moss lands. The crows began cawing wildly.

"Where is it?"

The bear took a heavy step toward Alice, who didn't flinch when he bent his massive head down, breathing her in. "In time, my King. In time. First, I need something in return."

"Why should I give you anything? You stole from me."

Yar huffed. I took a step toward them, keeping my sword at the ready but not quite in a threatening position as the crows circled above us, still frantic.

"You would never have come here if I hadn't sent the crows to steal your crown," he said.

Alice was quiet for a moment, considering his words, then replied: "What is it that you want?"

The bear turned his body a half-step and lifted his back leg, so we could see that it was caught in the menacing grip of an iron trap shaped like the head of a swamp demon, the bear's paw in its open mouth and its nail-like teeth puncturing the fur. Blood poured from the wounds like a river leaking through a dam about to burst. Alice rushed under the bear and cradled his leg in her arms.

"Can you remove it?" Yar asked.

"I can try," Alice said, examining the contraption for a release. "Lady Nora, can you come help with this?"

I looked up. There were small breaks in the branches where stars came into focus. We had minutes, maybe, before the sun set and the bell rang.

"Lady Nora!"

Alice tried prying the thing open, blood sliding down her arms to stain her white shirt while Yar growled in pain. What was the point? I wondered. It minutes this would all be over, and we would be on our way home to eat dinner and do our math homework.

"Nora!"

I shook my thoughts away and rushed over, putting my sword down on the moss, and sliding my fingers in between the trap's teeth where it was warm and sticky.

"On three," Alice said.

"One," I started.

"Two."

"Three." We both pulled at the trap, forcing its jaw apart. It took a while but eventually the thing snapped and fell open in two pieces.

Yar lift his paw away and turned toward Alice. "Thank you," he bowed his head. "My King."

Alice reached up to touch the bear's muzzle. Just as her fingers brushed against his nose, the bell rang far in the distance. The weight of the sword lifted from my hand as the blood bear and his crows dissolved into the misty air.

We found her crown of twigs resting against a nearby tree. Alice placed it back on her head and smiled. "Let's go home."

#

It was all the same as I remembered it. The house, the driveway, the barn nearly falling over in the backyard. I'm not sure what I was expecting until I was there, staring up at the windows that used to be my own. I did not expect it to be so familiar. Though the dirty windshield, it was like seeing an old home movie on a faded television screen, like it existed somewhere held in time.

"We have to limit visits to an hour. Otherwise, the radiation could be a problem." He handed me a plastic bag like the ones police on TV shows use to bag up evidence at crime scenes. I guessed that was kind of what this place was.

My whole family died here when the plant exploded, though my sister was still considered missing, with so many others whose bodies were never recovered. I was away at college in Michigan when it happened. That phone call changed my life.

I walked toward the front door, as I had a thousand times as a child. I felt that deep weight pulling on my lung as my fingers wrapped around the doorknob. This was where my parents' bodies were found. My dad in the kitchen, making tea; my mother in the study correcting term papers. I swallowed. I wanted to remember this place as it was before and not what it had become over the years of decay and abandonment. I wanted to turn around then, go back to the truck, and ask Lewis to take me away.

My grip on the knob tightened. No. I came here to do what the police, the army, and their packs of dogs had failed to do all these years: find Alice. Because I knew what they couldn't know. I twisted the knob

160

and pushed the door open, stepping into the house for the first time, and the last time.

#

"The old kings are buried in the roots of the elder tree," Alice said, placing her hand on the trunk of the massive tree. It was so big that Alice and I could both wrap our arms around it and our fingers wouldn't touch. The old tree was deep in the middle of the forest, nestled into a ravine.

"How do you know?" I asked.

"Because I can feel their spirits inside." She took my hand and pressed my palm against the red bark. "Close your eyes."

"I don't feel anything."

"You're not even trying, Lady Nora."

I closed my eyes and breathed in the warm summer air. I was turning seventeen in five days. I had just graduated high school. And despite the very real feeling of the sword in my hand and the bark under my fingers, I was beginning to wonder how much any of this mattered. I had a college acceptance letter sitting open on the kitchen table: another world was calling to me, a very different one than that our childhood games.

Alice was going to be nineteen that fall. She had never even applied to college. She was working at the local grocery store part-time and spent the rest of her time here in the woods.

"Yes, I think I can feel them now," I lied.

"See?" Alice smiled. "So, when I die, you are going to bury me here."

I pulled my hand away from hers and stepped back from the tree. "Why are we talking about this?"

"Just promise me that you will."

"No," I said. "Don't you want to be buried with Mom and Dad? Or what if you get married or have children? They won't want to bury you out by this tree."

"I am your King and I demand it," she said.

"You're my sister," I said, "not a King."

Alice silently stared at me, betrayed.

Sensing a shift, I looked down to the thing in my hand which was no longer a sword, but just a simple birch branch. And when I put it in the crook of the tree that night, it was for the last time.

#

It wasn't my house anymore. Nothing about this place, everything covered in white sheets, reminded me of the home I grew up in. I was relieved in a way, but also disappointed. I put the plastic bag down on the counter and walked outside, through the back door.

I stood at the edge of the woods, looking into the break in the trees where Alice and I always entered the morning before our next adventure. I wanted this time to be like all the times that came before. But it wasn't.

The birch branch was still there in the crook of the tree, untouched, as if it had been waiting for me to return all these years. The twig crown was gone, however.

I reached in for the branch, wanted to feel it in my hands again, one last time. When my fingers brush it, the branched changed. I pulled it out of the tree and held it out in front of me, feeling the familiar weight of the sword in my hands.

"Hey! Put that back. It does not belong to you."

My arm went limp, nearly dropping the weapon. I turned to face a young woman, wearing her glittering golden crown on her head.

"Alice…" I took a step toward her, but she reflexively took a step backward. She looked exactly as she had the day I left for college.

"Who are you? How did you find this place?"

"Alice, it's me. It's Nora."

"Lady Nora is gone," she said, still backing away from me.

"I'm not, I'm here."

"She left many years ago."

"But I came back."

"You're not Lady Nora."

I knelt in the leaves, thrust the tip of my sword into the ground, and bowed my head. My voice shook as I said the words: "You are my King, and I am your knight. I swore to protect you until the end of my days."

I looked up as Alice took a hesitant step forward, her head tilting back and forth, studying my face. She reached out and walked her fingers along my hairline, down my jaw, and cupped my face in her palms. "Lady Nora," she said finally. "Where have you been?"

I clasped a hand over hers. "I'm so sorry that I left," I said, my eyes welling with tears that threatened to spill out down my cheeks and into her hands. She put her arms around my neck and pulled me closer.

She smelled of the night air and silty moss, as though she was part of the forest now.

"You're here now," she said.

I pulled back and looked into her eyes. "I'm here now."

She was quiet for a moment, and then said: "I would like to show you something."

I followed Alice into the woods, away from the house, along the path that hugged the edge of the cliffs for a little over a mile. The heavy fog was lifting from the forest.

As I watched Alice weaving her way gracefully along the path, stepping over fallen logs and ducking under low-hanging branches, her crown glowing in the light, my head started feeling light. I knew what I was seeing must not be real: it was probably the poison gas filling my head with hallucinations, and I would die out here in the woods. But maybe it was real enough; maybe I could stay here and protect Alice like I was always supposed to, like I promised her I would.

I knew where we were going before we set foot on the path: the elder tree. I saw its red bark through the green of the pines as we got closer, ascending into the sky, so high that its top could not even be seen from the forest floor.

We climbed down the rocks into the ravine where the giant roots of the tree rose from the ground like tentacles and grappled onto the rock walls around them. Alice led me to the base of the tree, where a small opening led underneath the roots to a small cavern.

She pointed to the opening and I knelt in front of it, peering through the child-sized opening. In the darkness, leaning up against the side of the cave under the roots, was a human skeleton. Its bones pure white, the clothing rotting away in patches and hanging off its rib cage. I looked at Alice, who stared me.

"Do you know who that is?

I looked at the bones and saw the circlet of twigs and red ribbon adorned on its head. "Of course," I said. "It's my King."

"Do you know what happened?"

"A chemical accident, ten years ago." I turned around to face her.

"No, that wasn't it," she said quietly. "Do you remember the first witch?"

I thought for a moment. It was a name I hadn't heard in a long time. "She tried to take the kingdom," I said, remembering one of our earliest adventures. "We fought her at the plains, at the edge of the woods, and you banished her from the forest."

"Yes." Alice walked to the skeleton and knelt before it, staring at the empty sockets where her eyes used to be. "When you left, she came back, knowing that I was vulnerable. Unprotected. She used the sap of the elder tree for one of her spells. It was only supposed to kill me, but…"

"It killed everyone else, too," I said.

"Do you remember what I asked you before you left?"

I nodded. "You asked me to bury your body in the roots of the elder tree, like all the Kings that came before."

"Will you help me?"

Together, we dug a hole in the ground between the roots with our hands. Piece by piece we carried her bones into the grave and reassembled them so that her arms were crossed against her chest.

I placed the twig crown on her hands and then we buried her in the earth.

"I'm so sorry, Alice. I was supposed to protect you."

Alice's expression was somber in the fading light. "But you did. For a long time. And then you left because you don't really belong here."

"I want to stay this time."

"You can't. The first witch's spell is still cursing this forest; it will kill you if you stay."

"What is a knight without her King?" I asked, feeling the tears coming back to my eyes.

"Someone with another life that will miss her if she doesn't return." Alice took my hand and laid it on the trunk of the elder tree. "Do you feel that?"

I held my breath and waited. My fingers hummed and I felt the tree pulse, like a small heartbeat under my fingertip. I closed my eyes. I saw Alice, standing on the edge of the cliffs, looking out across the lower forest, her golden crown glittering in the sun.

"Thank you for keeping your promise, Lady Nora." she whispered in my ear.

When I opened my eyes, Alice was gone.

\#

I walked out of the woods alone, leaving the branch in the crook where it belonged.

Inside the house, I picked up the plastic bag and walked slowly toward the front. This time, I saw what I hadn't seen before. My mother's art still hung on the wall—the watercolors of the garden in spring—the book my father was reading still lay open on the kitchen counter, the page dog-eared marking his spot. I thought about picking it up and bringing it with me, but I couldn't bear to touch anything, to change anything, about what had been before. I wasn't here to change the past.

I left the house with the empty bag and climbed back into the truck with Lewis. He looked at me with a raised eyebrow. "You didn't take anything?"

I looked down at the empty bag in my hands but said nothing.

"Are you ready to go? We need to get back before dark."

I nodded. "Yes, let's go."

He started the engine and pulled out of the driveway and back out onto the main road. "I'm sorry you didn't find what you were looking for," Lewis said.

I watched my old house and the forest beyond disappear into the rearview mirror. From the dark trees far behind, a giant bear emerged with Alice on his back, her crown glowing in the waning light.

**Jess Ko** is a speculative fiction author from an island off the coast of New England. She is a recent graduate of the Stonecoast MFA program. Her fiction has appeared in *Metaphorosis*, *Ghost Parachute*, and others.

# Mr. Regret
## by R.A. Clarke

I was drunk. Not the good kind either. Whiskey did this to me every time, turned me into a blubbering black hole of self-pity and depression. Nothing short of a miracle could break me out of this funk.

The night started out like it always did. I slathered makeup on my face, styled my hair just right, and squeezed my few-too-many pounds into a revealing little number. All to attract a still-single-but-not-a-loser member of the opposite sex. A rare species in my current age bracket.

I went to the usual club with a couple of girlfriends from work. They were single and hunting, just like I was. We danced flamboyantly and more than a little too sexy, hoping Mr. Right would be drawn in by sheer animal magnetism. I scoped the room, unenthused by the candidates, but perhaps tonight would be that one night I'd discover a diamond in the rough. I always told myself that.

There were no diamonds.

Instead, I met Nick and Jimmy, who undoubtedly still lived in their parents' basements, praying to finally lose their virginity to a real woman.

"Did you know that video gaming can cause carpal tunnel?" Jimmy had asked.

I doubted it was the video games that did that.

Christian cha-cha'd into our circle next, with awkward finger pointing and a tan line where his ring normally resided for goodness sakes. A real slick-haired smooth-talker looking for an easy lay. I mean, I'm desperate, but not that desperate.

By midnight we'd had enough. I decided to walk home, waving goodnight to my friends as they got into a taxi. My apartment was a fair distance away, fifteen minutes on foot, but I figured the cool autumn air might do me good. Or it wouldn't, and I'd simply catch pneumonia and die. That worked too. *Boy, the whisky is really working its magic tonight.*

I popped into a 24-hour convenience store to buy a chocolate bar. My drug of choice. Wandering down the aisle, the latest edition of Architect Magazine stood out to me. I winced. There he was—his damn face right on the cover. Looking as sexy as ever with his perfectly groomed goatee and salt n' pepper hair. Jason Whitfield. Father time had been kind to him.

Twenty-two years ago, I remember how perfect things had been…. I was young and perky, just finishing up a hard-earned University degree, bright-eyed and raring to go. Not to mention being thirty-five pounds lighter. Jason was my boyfriend, the man of my dreams, my Mr. Right. We were meant for each other, but then I had to go and mess it all up. Something made me break up with him, but I couldn't for the life of me, imagine what that might've been. I was so stupid back then. Too naive to realize what I'd lost until it was too late.

I snatched the magazine off the rack and thrust a few bills at the cashier, already biting into a Mars bar. Voracious for creature comfort, there was another stuffed in my pocket for later.

I stumbled my way down the sidewalk, a few too many drinks sloshing around inside me. Staring at the magazine riled up the bitterness. I heard Jason was still single, hailed as one of the most eligible bachelors in the country. Last year I sent him an email, thinking we could rekindle the romance. Maybe he missed me too?

I never received a response.

What did it even matter at this point? Really. I had a cat who hated me, a job I dreaded going to, and the only romance I ever experienced was on the television screen. Unless I counted the frequent and rhythmic banging emanating from next door. From the muffled accompanying moans and whimpers, it was clear my neighbor had no lack of romance in *his* life. I tried not to feel jealous when I listened in, popcorn in hand. What was wrong with me?

The only thing that brought me joy in this shit life was my mom, and she passed away six months ago. She was the only one who gave a crap about me. Honestly, I don't know why I didn't just end it all then. It's been so hard without her.

Thinking back, I can pinpoint the day that everything started to go downhill. It was June 16th, 1997. The day I walked away from a millionaire.

And it just kept rolling from there.

Nearing the river, I wiped at the tears and melting mascara as a fresh sob racked my shoulders. Jason was the one that got away. The one I *let* get away.

Twenty-two years had passed, spent dreaming of what might have been. Too many long years of regret, every moment of it leading me here. Balling my eyes out, I sit on the ledge of a single lane bridge only a few short minutes from my house.

It wasn't as impressive or scenic a locale as I'd imagined for my grand exit, nor was the bridge a beautiful feat of engineering mastery, but it was plenty high to be effective. Tonight, that was enough for me.

Railroad tracks leading to unknown places stretched out below, soon to be decorated with a warm shade of red.

"I am over this!" I cried out into the stillness. "I'm done." I set my jaw firm in my decision. It was time to end the madness.

I pulled off my high heels, setting them aside on the sidewalk. No need to damage a perfectly good pair of *Jimmy Choo's*. Standing up, I leaned back against the rail, clutching it as an abnormally strong gust of wind tested my balance. Seconds later, another wave of air crashed over me, blowing my hair and clothes like a flag in the prairies. Was a storm moving in? It had been calm all night until now. Looking up, nothing but stars twinkled above.

Not a hint of a cloud. *Odd.*

"Enough distractions Linda," I ordered myself with a head shake. It was time to get back to the task at hand. "Let's just get this over with. The world will be thankful," I muttered. A fresh batch of tears streamed down my cheeks as I stared at the ground, preparing for the fall. My mind spun, thinking about all the things I didn't get to do, all the ways I wasted my existence, and how nothing I could do would ever make it right again. My grip slowly loosened, the cold metal railing sliding beneath my fingertips.

"Are you sure you want to do that?"

Startled by the deep voice behind me, my hands flexed in shock. As I reclaimed my hold, I glanced over my shoulder to see who was there. Heart pounding, I felt vulnerable, exposed. Fear took control as I saw a strange man standing there. A tall, sharply dressed man only feet away. His hands were tucked into his pockets as he calmly smiled.

*He could have a knife in his pocket.*

"Stay back! Get away from me." I turned my body against the rails to face the intruder, eyes trained on him. The man put his hands up, both empty.

"I mean you no harm, Linda."

"How do you know my name?" Hooking an elbow around one of the metal rails, I frantically dug through my purse. My fingertips finally touched a cylindrical container of pepper spray. Like American Express, I never leave home without it. "Just back off!" I wanted to die in my own way, on my own terms. Not at the hands of some pervy, stalker serial killer.

As I whipped out the cannister, my foot simultaneously slipped off the edge, jarring my body downward. A splice of a scream escaped my lips before I felt two firm hands grab my shoulders. Pervy stalker man's gaze locked with mine, his eyes focused and unwavering. The steady support allowed my foot to regain purchase on the cold concrete.

"I'm not going to hurt you," he soothed. "Come now." He nodded toward the safe side where he stood. Taking my hand, I was guided back over the rails.

Once my feet were back on the sidewalk, my heart rate slowing, I couldn't help but notice his striking features. The bluest eyes I had ever seen, a crisp, pointed nose, and a meticulously trimmed beard that faded into his sideburns. He had two streaks of colour in his dark wavy hair, one white and one red, each running parallel to the other, running back from his hairline. A curious style choice.

"Who are you?" I asked shakily, suddenly feeling the nighttime chill on my skin. Or maybe I was in shock.

"I am a friend. My name is irrelevant."

His smile was alarmingly charming. Some of my fear ebbed.

"Oh, no it is *very* relevant. Who are you?" I managed a weak smile looking into those ice-blue eyes, and unable to help myself, I added, "And are you single?"

The man chuckled, shaking his head. "I don't have any interest in women."

*Ohhh… got it.* That made sense, with the nice clothes and meticulous grooming. "Sorry, I hope I didn't offend you. I actually know a couple of guys from the gym that would love to meet you, I'm sure."

"Uh, no, I have no interest in men either. I don't date, but thank you for asking." He let me go, watching to be certain I was stable. I didn't feel particularly steady, my body still trembling from the experience, but my mind felt sharper now. The alcoholic depression was rapidly clearing from my thoughts. I glanced back over the side of the bridge, contemplating what nearly happened. Oddly, I felt a mixture of relief and sadness.

"What are you doing here? It's like 3:00am. Are you going to kill me?"

"Isn't that what you want? To die?"

The fear rose within me again, despite his temperate expression. My limbs stiffened, preparing to run as I stepped back. "That's my business." I raised the pepper spray still locked in my hand, preparing to squirt and run. "Nobody wants to be *murdered*."

He raised his hands again, shaking his head. "I am not here to kill you. I heard your distress and I've come to offer you a solution. An option."

My face twisted in confusion. "What?"

"If you had the chance to go back to do one thing over again, would you take it?"

*What?* My brain hurt.

"Listen buddy, I think you need to head back to your padded room, okay?"

His eyes twinkled with amusement as he raised a hand, snapping his fingers. I squinted as a blinding light flashed, white-washing all of our surroundings. The light faded just as quickly, but when my vision reacclimated, I was not where I should've been. Warm air enveloped me, easing the goose bumps from my exposed skin.

*Where the hell am I?*

"This is the hallway of decisions." The man announced, still standing in front of me. Slipping his hands back in his pockets, he grinned. "*Your* hallway to be exact."

"Undo it." I looked around, panicking. This was too bizarre to be real. I stood in the middle of a long yellow hallway—so yellow it could squeeze lemon. The blazing citrus walls were lined with old wooden doors, the heavy kind you don't find in stores anymore. "Undo it now. Take me back. Do the snappy thing again." My heart was pounding a drum solo in my chest.

"Let me explain first. When I'm done, if you still want to return to the bridge, I will most definitely take you back." He spread his arms wide then, palms up. "Deal?"

I couldn't believe what was happening. Is this Heaven, or maybe Hell? Did I jump already and not remember? Or maybe this guy attacked and drugged me, and I was trapped in his twisted torture chamber. My eyes darted all around, trying to make sense of it all. The urge to run swelled, but I had no clue where I was.

My gaze flitted back to he-who-shall-not-be-named, who continued to regard me calmly. Hands back in his pockets, he leaned forward, meeting my gaze. I tried to look away, but found I couldn't. It was like an emotional shift was forced upon me, an irresistible pull commanding my attention. Something soft glimmered in his eyes, hypnotic and inviting. My heartbeat slowed and my nerves eased. This fantastical stranger was urging me to trust him, and I was listening.

"Relax," he cooed softly, gaze steady.

"Okay," I said on a breathy sigh.

After a moment of silence passed, his pacifying demeanor shifted dramatically.

"Great." He straightened, clapping his hands together cheerfully. The man's entire expression brightened as he genially guided me forward. He'd make an excellent hotel manager.

*What a quirky guy.*

"These are the doors of regret." He pointed down the hallway. "Everybody's doors are different. Some have too many to count, while others only have one or two."

"Doors of regret," I repeated skeptically, brows furrowed. I counted seven doors in total, spread out down the hall.

"That's right, and these are *your* doors." He walked over to the first, plopping a hand onto the brass handle. He waved me closer, "Come on."

Eyes constantly scanning, I followed. "Is this some kind of elaborate prank? Are there hidden cameras around here somewhere?" I examined my surroundings, eyes squinting. "And can we do something about the blinding yellow walls?"

"Oh, yes of course." Raising his hand, he snapped his fingers once more. The paint rippled like a wave down the length of the hall, the colour fading into a pale shade of violet. "Is this better?"

Purple wasn't a particular favorite of mine, but it was definitely better than neon lemonade. "Yes, thank you."

"Very good." The consummate host, the man snapped his fingers yet again, opening the door this time. He peered inside briefly, before motioning for me to do the same. "Does this look familiar to you?" I followed his gaze, eyes widening in a double take.

It was the cafe I got a job waitressing in when I was 17. I practically grew up in that place, and it was right there in front of me, plain as day. "Incredible. Barny's burned down years ago." Wondering whether it was a screen or a hologram, I tried to wave a hand through the image, but the man quickly blocked me.

"No touching. Just watch," he encouraged.

I saw myself bussing a table, then head toward a booth to take an order. I cringed as I heard a telltale laugh ring out, like nails on a chalkboard. *Oh, I know when this is.*

Trudy, the owner of that horrible laugh, sat with all her popular flunkies. She was twittering on about how awesome her new car was (that her rich daddy bought), what jewelry she purchased recently, and the expensive clothing she wore. Trudy hated me, and I didn't particularly care for her either, since she constantly went out of her way to make my school experience as miserable as possible. I wasn't cool enough to breathe in her airspace.

"Oh look, its *Linda*. It makes sense *you* would be the one to serve me." She cackled, highlighting my low-class need to work. She proceeded to spell out her overly specific order, light on this and substitute this with that... and only glacier water in a bottle, with a straw. She was watching her figure before a big date with the quarterback, apparently. With a hair flip she asked pointedly, "Can you manage that Lin-*Duh*? And you better not screw it up. My dad can get you fired in a heartbeat."

I watched my younger self walk away seething. "Can I go in there?" I asked, stepping forward. Suddenly, I felt invigorated by what these doors might mean. A do-over. I knew what came next, so I wondered, how could I still mess with Trudy's head while simultaneously stopping my old self?

"Wait," he held an arm out, holding me back. The vision beyond the door fast forwarded like an old recorded VHS movie. Young Linda retrieved the order sitting on the pass bar. She took Trudy's plate into the back and promptly spit in the food when nobody was looking. I looked away embarrassed, cheeks turning red. My nameless guide raised an eyebrow.

"That wasn't my finest moment, I know." I shrugged. "I felt really bad after, too. That brief moment of satisfaction didn't last. Trudy was a bitch for sure, but stooping to that low was a huge stain on my otherwise ethical working life. The guilt has haunted me."

"And that is precisely why you are here. Now you understand more clearly what lies behind these doors. Each one contains one of your most impactful regrets. Things that you might want to do over if given the chance." He pulled the door closed.

"So, I can go back and change all of my regrets?"

"It doesn't quite work like that." He led me to the next door down the hall. This one had a silver doorknob. "There are some strings attached. I am offering you the option to relive *one* of your worst regrets. Only one. So, you must choose wisely."

"Why only one?"

"We will talk more. First, go ahead and check every door. However, do not walk through any of them yet." His face was very serious. "If you pass a threshold in any way, even if it's just a pinky finger, that becomes your choice. Once the decision is made, it cannot be undone."

"Okay…" I felt nervous turning the silver handle, but that feeling was quickly replaced with frustration when the door refused to budge. Uselessly, I tried again, then remembered all the finger-snapping this mysterious man was so very fond of.

"So, what, I just snap it open like you did?" I snapped my thumb and middle finger with gusto. Nothing happened. "Open sesame!" I commanded, giving it another try, to no avail.

The man shook his head, robust rumbles of laughter escaping his perfectly formed lips. "Leave the snapping to me, Linda. You will need to use the keys."

We stared at each other a moment. Then another. His smile remained placid, while mine twitched with growing confusion.

Finally, I broke the silence. "Um, so, are you going to give them to me?"

"You've had them all along." With his head, he nodded toward my purse.

"What?" My fingers began rummaging immediately. Sure enough, there was a metal ring with seven ornately designed keys on it. They were heavy like cast iron. How had I not noticed?

"Let me know when you've chosen," my guide added, then meandered off.

I turned back to the door, whispering, "Here we go." After trying six of the keys, I finally found the right one. Turning the silver handle, the latch clicked and the door swung open.

*Only one...*

I watched the scenes play out behind each successive door, cringing more and more as the experiences were revived before my eyes. The silver-handled door led to my junior high dance, when I'd exited the bathroom with a small piece of dress tucked in my underwear.

A pewter door knob opened into an important job interview ten years ago, when I'd broken down crying. So embarrassing.

The modern chrome knob revealed that time I ignored and walked past a homeless man in the middle of winter, then recognized him on the news the next day. He'd died. Giving him my extra coins might not have changed anything, but I always wondered *what if?*

I turned a crystal-like door handle and my cheeks flushed as I watched a seven-year-old me pumping fake coins into a gumball machine, nearly emptying the whole container before my backpack was full.

A golden knob highlighted the single time I forgot to put money into the lottery pool at work and they freaking won 150,000 dollars. Every day thereafter, I cursed at the copy of the lottery ticket they proudly pinned up in the staffroom. I was still kicking myself over that. *23 45 98 12 72.* To this day, I still see those lotto numbers in my head, burned into my subconscious. I've always had a good mind for numbers.

With each new door pull I held my breath, waiting to see him. Jason. But he hadn't shown up yet. Now, standing before the very last door I took a deep breath. This had to be it.

An ornately crafted wrought iron handle garnished the dark wooden door. I depressed the flat button lever on top, and pulled. Dim light shone on my face as I recognized the inside of Jason's car parked outside his apartment building. *This is it.* A much younger me sat in the passenger seat, feeling torn after going to dinner and a movie. Jason invited young Linda up to his place. She hemmed and hawed. He caressed her thigh and said he was falling in love, leaning over for a kiss, but young Linda stopped him.

"What are you doing you stupid cow!" I yelled through the doorway, but it made zero impact on the scene playing out. I watched as if I were sitting in the backseat.

Young Linda explained she couldn't continue seeing him, saying he was a great guy but she simply couldn't stay in the city after graduation. I saw Jason's face fall, then quickly grow irritated. He was angry about how the last few months were a giant waste of time. She offered to try long distance, but he didn't go for it. Jason said he couldn't live like that, not seeing her all the time. He begged her to just come up for one drink so they could talk about it more.

*He is perfect for you. You're blowing it!*

The naive idiot version of me just sat there, with her poker straight hair pulled into a ponytail, and an awkward expression on her face. She was wearing a very unfortunate jean jacket and flowery-skirt combo, still dressing true to her farm girl roots, contrary to popular styles of the time. Young Linda turned him down. He got angry and refused to drive her home, so she got out to walk.

"It's a wonder a guy like Jason was even interested in you at all," I muttered to myself. "He was so out of your league, yet wanted you anyway... and then you decided to blow him off." I growled. The vision faded to black and then restarted from the beginning. "He was in love with us for goodness sakes! You've never found another man as high caliber as him. And you never will."

I stopped myself. *Why am I standing here spouting off like this? I can change it.*

I waved to my silent observer down the hall.

In a single blink he appeared at my side. I stumbled back a step, surprised. "S-so, Mr. Regret man," *for lack of a better name,* "I've chosen. How does this work? I walk through, redo it all and then come back to see how my life turned out?" I imagined waking up next to Jason tomorrow morning. Maybe even having a couple kids running around the house.

"Mr. Regret... I like that." He smirked. "When you walk through the door you'll be back as you once were, reliving the moment you've just seen here." He motioned to the door. "But once you do, you can never return to your old life. As I said before, it cannot be undone."

"But what if I can't fix it? I don't get to try again, or just give up and resume my old life?"

"That is the conundrum. What happens beyond the door is out of my control. I am only able to give you the opportunity. The choice whether it's worth the risk is up to you. If you choose not to enter a doorway, I will take you back to the bridge."

"Does anybody ever say no?"

"The odd time."

"Why?"

"There are certain things they wouldn't dare change. Fear. Not worth the energy... There are many reasons." Mr. Regret shrugged.

I considered that information, letting it soak in. "Why did you pick me?"

"We screen for hopelessness," he replied matter-of-factly.

I wanted to be offended by that answer, but I *was* just about to throw myself off a bridge when we'd met. All things considered, hopeless seemed fairly appropriate.

"We?" I prodded.

"It's a big world, and I am but one being."

*Huh, so there are more like him.* "Are you an angel or something?"

He shot me a look belying tested patience, the first real emotion I'd seen from him yet. It didn't last long though, his demeanor quickly flipped back to the calm and soothing. "You may call me that if you wish. But not everyone will."

"Why—"

"Do you know what you'd like to do, or would you like a moment to think it over?" He cut me off, anticipating more questions.

I looked down at my hands, running all the pros and cons through my mind. A man who loves me and the endless possibilities that would come with that, versus the useless routine that I'm living now. What cons could there be? I had nothing to lose. Mr. Regret should already know that, otherwise he wouldn't have found me.

"I am walking through this door."

"Excellent. Best of luck to you." His smile was broad, hands clasped behind his back.

I turned back to the door, pumping myself up inside. *I can't believe this is really happening.* Just as I moved my leg across the threshold, Mr. Regret piped up again.

"Oh, one other tiny little thing. There is always a side effect from the continuum shift. Usually very minor. Nothing to worry about." He breezed through that statement very quickly, then waved me onward, charming smile unfazed.

With one leg in, and one leg out, I had concerns. "Wait, what kind of side effe—" But my train of thought was lost mid-sentence as a powerful force grabbed onto my limb. It was like quicksand, sucking me deeper into the doorway. Panic filled every crevice of my body as I looked frantically to my nameless recruiter for assistance. My eyes felt so wide, my eyebrows probably touched my hairline.

"It's normal. Don't fight it. Just let it take you where you want to go."

It didn't feel safe. Like I was on the wrong end of an industrial-strength vacuum cleaner. My other leg was being pulled in now. "Are you telling me the truth?"

"Don't be afraid, Linda." He rested his hand on the door knob, preparing to close it behind me. "Best wishes in your new life."

My hips were being sucked in. I leaned forward, my heart racing. Had I been duped? Could this be some kind of experimental device that is slowly sucking the life out of me? I had major second thoughts, but I doubted I had a choice in the matter anymore. My chance to bolt was too far gone. My waist was suctioned in, the rib cage next on the docket. I suddenly remembered my question and spat it out again. "What kind of side effects?"

"Oh, yes. Usually it's just a minor change in your body, or on rare occasions, a foreign object somewhere inside you."

"*What?* You should really tell people this stuff up front, seriously!" I was appalled. "Like a *large* foreign object?"

187

My chest was being dragged in deeper and my mind was frantic, my breathing shallow.

"No, very small. Always removable by doctors."

I screamed involuntarily as my shoulders were pulled in, the forceful energy now grasping at my arms too.

But I didn't feel any pain, which was promising. Maybe it would be okay after all. Mr. Regret was still standing there, watching and smiling at me so encouragingly. I mean, he saved me before, so he can't be evil. *Right?* My internal monologue helped to battle my rampant worst-case-scenario thoughts. Slightly.

Mr. Regret leaned over to lock eyes with me, his mystical gaze working hard to soothe. Once more I couldn't look away, and instantly felt my body relax. It seemed to be his special power, and at this moment, I was thankful for the relief. That familiar shimmer appeared in his irises again, and then his face was gone. My head sank through the doorway and everything disappeared from view.

\#

I opened my eyes; head feeling a little fuzzy. Looking down I saw my 23-year-old body sitting in the passenger seat, ankles crossed, the flowery skirt draped over my thighs. I lifted my hands to inspect them, wiggling my fingers, in awe that I was in control.

*It really happened. I'm really here.*

grinning. If he were a cartoon right then, I'm sure there would be a twinkling star on his teeth. The extra bedroom he used as his drafting room, the walls covered with plans and blueprints, and a drawing table at one end. He was studying to become an architect with his father's firm, and clearly *very* determined to follow in his notable footsteps. Jason's family was quite well off.

The last stop was his bedroom, filled with modern decor (well, modern for 1997), the style very chic. His bed was covered by a masculine grey comforter, sleek and silky-smooth. I assumed he must have a hired cleaner, as not many single men I knew cared about arranging throw pillows. He waved his arms grandly as we walked in, announcing, "This is where the magic happens." Never mind the room, his smile was magical.

"This is a real bachelor pad," I commented with a laugh. "A very impressive place."

"Thanks. Yeah, I guess it is a bit of a 'pad'. But I just haven't found the right girl yet. It needs a feminine touch, don't you think?" He slipped behind me, nuzzling my neck as his arms wrapped around my waist. I felt my heart flutter, and something else too. He spun me in his arms, his mouth falling onto mine, fingers wrapping in my hair. I was a bit surprised by the aggressive sexuality. Jason had always been a sweetheart without fail, so this was a whole new side of his personality.

"Whoa, let's not rush things," I took a step back. He looked irritated for a split second, but it vanished quickly. He held my hands, laughing at his own enthusiasm like an embarrassed schoolboy.

"I'm sorry, I am just so into you Linda, I can't help myself. You are everything I've ever wanted in a woman." Jason stepped closer again, his eyes locking with mine as he caressed my cheek. "I am falling in love with you."

And there they were… the words I had wanted to hear again for twenty-two painful years. This was the man of my dreams, standing before my very eyes. Without a second thought, I threw myself into his arms, kissing him passionately. This deal was getting sealed tonight. He had no idea what he was in for. I was going to rock his world.

# 

The morning came too soon. A soft billowy light cascaded in from the windows, as I opened my eyes and ran a hand through my thoroughly disheveled hair. Last night had been better than any daydream I'd ever had. Jason was a rocket in the sack, full of endless energy, and very enthusiastic. Almost overly so at times. He knew his way around a woman, I could tell, but most of his focus remained on his own pleasure. That was not uncommon in my experience. *We can work on that,* I thought with a smile. *It was our first night together after all, there's plenty of time to work out the kinks.*

Where was that love of mine? Jason's side of the bed was empty. I crawled out from under the crumpled sheets, finding my clothing to get dressed. As I pulled on my skirt, I noticed something was very different about my right foot. *Holy shit!* I had a sixth toe. An extra little pinky toe stuck onto the end.

I wiggled it. Well at least now I knew what my side effect was. I should have felt more horrified, but instead I found myself thankful I didn't have a third eye, or a tennis ball in my butt cheek or something. I could handle a toe. *Plastic surgery here I come.*

I peered out the bedroom door to see Jason sitting in a pedestal chair at the kitchen island, sipping on a coffee. He wore a dapper looking outfit, suit pants and dress shirt, as if he was heading to a job interview.

"Good morning handsome," I greeted with a smile, looking forward to a brand-new day.

"Good morning. Do you want some coffee for the road?" He turned his head and asked, returning a more polite smile.

"For the road?" I walked up and wrapped my arms around his chest from behind, kissing him on the cheek. "I thought maybe we could grab some breakfast."

"Oh man, I can't. My father called me into work. He wants me to sit in on an important meeting to learn the ropes." He slipped out of my arms and walked to the coffee pot. He filled up a *Styrofoam* go-cup, snapping a lid on top. *Who keeps go-cups in their apartment?*

"You disappeared on me this morning. I'd hoped for some morning cuddles," I winked, taking the cup he offered. I moved in for a kiss.

"Yeah," he stepped back, hands settling on his hips. "About that, listen… last night was fun." He reached to grab his suit jacket draped over the back of the stool. My smile faded, sensing something wasn't quite right. His temperature was cool as he regarded me, not his usual self at all.

"It was. Very much so," I agreed, brows raised waiting for him to continue.

"But I just don't think *this*," he waved his hand between us, "is working for me."

"What?" I was shocked and confused. My pulse pounded. "But you said you were falling in love with me last night." How does a person flip their feelings so quickly? They don't.

"I say a lot of things to get what I want." He adjusted his cuffs and lapels, very business-like.

"So that was a lie? Was it all a lie?"

"You have this innocent farm girl thing going on that I found irresistible. I just had to try a sample." His lips twitched, amused.

"Sample?" I was incredulous, an instant heat flaming my cheeks. *I'm some kind of bizarre conquest?* "But we've dated for months!"

"You're a tough nut to crack, admittedly. It took way more time and effort than I imagined."

"How dare you!" I flew at him and his smug little smirk. He grabbed my wrists and pushed me back. I stumbled but straightened myself right away, glaring at him.

Jason smoothed down his hair. "No need for theatrics. Men sleep with women, it's the way of the world. You didn't have to say yes last night. Own up to your own sexuality, will you?" He headed to the front door, tossing my jean jacket over to me.

"You're trying to put this back on *me*? You shouldn't have lied! Saying you loved me... You manipulated me, used me. I didn't sign up for that." I was so angry I was shaking.

Jason shrugged. "Well, it went how it went. Can't go back now. There's no point in dwelling on things you can't change."

His words smacked me in the face. So callous and uncaring. Devoid of basic humanity or empathy. And devilishly ironic, given the situation.

I was finally seeing him for who… or what, he really was. His true colors. Jason wasn't the ungettable get, or the key to a dreamy pampered life. No, he was an asshole. An entitled, rich boy, clearly living only for his own selfish adventures. *How did I not pick up on this before?* My mind spun. *Or maybe I did… I did break up with him twenty-two years ago, after all. Had I sensed something was off back then?*

"You have no idea what I've been through for you. You were the one that got away." I growled, "How stupid am I?"

194

Jason looked confused. "What are you talking about?" He shook his head, scoffing.

I was a different girl when this first happened, with big dreams and high moral fiber. Thinking back on it now, I clearly must've picked up on this slimy part of him. But why didn't I remember the specifics? *Perhaps I blocked it all out.* In my aging desperation, was it possible I let the torture of that unexplained 'what if' taint my logic over time?

He opened the door, motioning for me to walk through it. Another damn door. "Thanks for a pleasant evening. Take care," he said, straight-faced. I picked up my go-cup.

I was so mad at him, but equally mad at myself. I actually walked through that damn quicksand door for this useless excuse for a man.

*No point in dwelling on the things you can't change,* he'd said. Begrudgingly, I admitted how right he'd been. That's exactly what I'd done for a large chunk of my life, dwelling on an unknown and letting it fester, boring a hole right through me. I'd let the experience rule me rather than shape me in moving forward.

"Come on, I need to leave soon." He waved faster, impatient.

I hurled my coffee at him with my dominant farmgirl throwing arm. Jason tried to dodge it but couldn't. I heard the lid pop off as it connected with his torso, brown liquid splashing down his shirt and pants. He squealed, feeling the heat. As the wet stain grew, soaking into the fibers of his no-doubt expensive outfit, a smile spread across my face. That felt slightly better.

"Oh no, I hope you're not *late*." I stomped past Jason, pushing him back against the door on my way by. He lashed out, clamping a hand onto my wrist, squeezing hard. He stared me down, his jaw flexing as his teeth clenched.

The intensity of his eyes jarred me.

"Let me go! Or would you like an assault charge to tarnish your daddy's image of you?" I matched his glare, deciding not to back down. I could tell he was fighting to contain his temper, or whatever other urges existed there. Was he capable of worse?

Worry began to seep in just as his hand released me, fingers popping open as if spring-loaded, lowering to clench into a fist by his side. The look on his face was disturbing, dark. I spun on my heel and stalked briskly down the hall, getting the hell away from him. When I didn't hear footsteps behind me as I rushed down the stairs, my relief swelled. Reaching safety was my first priority, and then maybe having a stiff drink.

Once I was out of the building and standing on the sidewalk, out of the danger zone, I let out a huge breath, expelling the many uncomfortable emotions pent up inside my body. My heart and my head ached, while my pulse was still in the process of slowing.

*Well that didn't go the way I thought. No wonder he's still single 22 years from now.*

This is exactly why some people don't call Mr. Regret an angel, I mused, remembering his earlier comment. Doing a mistake over again doesn't mean it's going to offer a better result. Sometimes it will turn out badly. *Like now.*

"So, I'm officially stuck here," I muttered to myself. "I have to live my useless old life all over again. Every shitty depressing part of it. No perfect man. No sunny future to look forward to." I sighed, staring down at my sixth toe, clad in a simple leather sandal. "And no *Jimmy Choo's.*"

*But, I'm young and skinny again… so there's that.* I shrugged.

My body felt dirty, in much need of a shower. Knowing what I know now, that asshole's germs would easily glow beneath a blacklight. It was imperative I wash all traces of Jason from my body immediately.

I started walking toward my old apartment… well, it wasn't so old anymore. In this timeline I'd just moved in from the University residence last year. Nothing was past tense anymore. *I'm in it. This is now. Again.*

Tears welled in my eyes, as the full weight of my error crashed down upon me. Furiously, I blinked the wetness away. "I should have just returned to the bridge."

But then a thought popped into my brain. My life doesn't have to be as bad as before, does it? I grudgingly acknowledged that I'd let a lot of crappy things occur, usually because I was stuck wallowing about the past, which cumulatively drove me to hopelessness. Couldn't I

197

simply make better decisions from this point on? If I did that, all those things that plagued me before wouldn't afflict me now. Well, not all of them anyway.

I had closure on Jason, at least. An unfortunate kind, but closure nonetheless.

*Why did I let the "what if's" drive me so crazy?*

"That kind of thinking stops right now, Linda," I thrust out a stern fist, giving myself a serious pep-talk.

Forcing myself to think positively was helping. I actually felt some hope. My mood continued to lighten, and I glanced at my surroundings with a whole new tint on the lens.

This turn of events didn't have to be horrible, because I wouldn't *let* it be horrible. I now had the benefit of all my life experience to guide me.

*Wait...*

My eyes widened in sudden realization.

*23 45 98 12 72.*

I dug a pen out of my purse and scribbled the numbers, just in case another random side effect decided to hit and I lost my memory or something. I also jotted down the exact date I lost out on that damn work lottery. "Thank goodness I've always had a good mind for numbers."

A slow smile spread on my lips.

Maybe Mr. Regret was an angel after all.


**R.A. Clarke** is a former police officer turned stay-at-home mom living in Portage la Prairie, Manitoba. She survives on sloppy toddler kisses, copious amounts of coffee, and immersing her mind in fantastical worlds of her own creation. Whenever not crafting short stories, she keeps busy working on her novel and writing/illustrating children's literature. R.A. Clarke's work has been published by the Writers Workout, Writers Weekly (24-hour contest 1st and 2nd place winner), Sirens Call Publications, and Polar Borealis Magazine. www.rachaelclarkewrites.com.

## The Princess in the Tower
## by S. E. White

As they fought through the toe-slicing shards of volcanic leavings scattered about the accursed valley, Sir Constans pulled off the last piece of his armor.

The greave *clinked* against glassy rock. Neither he nor Sir Infaustus looked to see where it fell. It didn't really matter. One foot followed after the other, while he disregarded the ache radiating up from his battered feet. His right arm trembled and shook, so beyond exhaustion he'd lost all control of the muscles.

He wouldn't be able to raise the sword sheathed at his side.

Dirt, runnels of sweat, and rusty streaks of blood smeared his smallclothes, flashing in and out of his vision with each step. *Dearest, blessed God, it will feel good to touch the river again.*

They had left their soft green camp two days ago. *Just two days!* All eighteen men together had taken less than a day to navigate the maze of twisted obsidian that covered the sandy valley between them and the castle that was their goal. Less than a day when they were hearty and whole, looking forward to nothing but satisfaction. Another rescue, another monster killed, another damsel saved, and the continued adulation of the kingdom.

Faces swam in front of his eyes, melting and reforming. Sir Fortis's sturdy chin and short, ruddy hair. Dark, sly eyes appeared to him, revealed in a twist of black rock. Those laughing black eyes had belonged to Sir Tenax. Before they were plucked out.

So clearly did he see his fellows that the hellscape around him vanished. The next shard nearly turned his ankle.

"We should have made sure," said Sir Infaustus.

Sir Constans blinked the visions of the dead away. He glanced sidelong at Infaustus and then turned his eyes back to watch his tricky footing. "No one else is left," he said flatly. "Only we two."

"As we ran, I thought I heard Sir Audens. Just by the door. I'll never forgive myself if he was still alive, and we left him there." Infaustus weaved into a boulder, thumped against it heavily, righted his course, and walked on. "We never . . . never leave a companion . . . behind." His words were interrupted by his stumbles. He had kept his breastplate on, scratched and filthy as it was.

Sunlight reflected off of it, spearing Sir Constans's eyes. Heat pounded into the top of his bared head. Dark as they were, somehow the rocks threw back the light in shining waves. The very ground, covered in flecks and sparkles, hurt to look at. Nothing here was kind. Nothing in this blasted land contained forgiveness.

They should never have come. *Rescuing the Princess, be damned. Our pride be damned. We surely were. Why would we think nothing of the fact that no one has returned from this quest, before? Why didn't I consider what that means?*

Mincing carefully down the nearest gully, Constans said, "As we ran, I s*aw* Sir Audens. She had him." *What was left of him.* "He was not alive. I give you my oath, Infaustus."

Infaustus only grunted in reply. Rather than try to clamber down the gully, he sat and slid to where Constans was waiting, favoring his left leg. Showers of small pebbles followed him, banging and clashing.

The leg was pleasantly cold, and numb, he had told Constans. At the castle she'd spat one clear stream of her venom at their fleeing figures, catching Infaustus. From the ragged smear on his thigh the poison still burrowed and twined.

"It's creeping," Infaustus said. "Farther up my leg. It's spreading. I can't—can't wipe it off." His voice shook.

Sir Constans stumbled over to help him up. "We have to keep going. We must. Get to camp." His voice was as exhausted as the rest of him. "Only a mile more. We'll . . . we'll find something to fix it, there." He gripped Infaustus's arm, hauled him back upright. The effort almost knocked him over.

He entertained a brief image of the two of them crossing the ground like jack-in-boxes, first one and then the other falling and being helped up. The silver-gray of his head, alternating with the curly brown of his fellow knight's. The image made him snort.

He rested a torn, bleeding palm on the nearest rock and leaned on it for support.

Head lowered, arms crossed tightly, Sir Infaustus stood in the dry bed of the gully. "She'll not let us go. We might say what we've seen." A drop of sweat fell from the tip of his nose. "Who will she devour, if no more knights come?"

Did his companion sway on his feet? Or was Sir Constans swaying? He blinked, shook his head, and took a few steps away from the rock. "If we are quick enough, she'll have no choice. Come."

Infaustus shook his head. Muddy brown hair, dark with sweat, clung to his neck and temples. "Sixteen men," he whispered. "All gone to that beautiful, beautiful monster."

Absolute silence surrounded them. At this time, yesterday, they had been approaching the castle together. Firm of purpose, determined to rescue the princess locked away there. To prove that they were, indeed, the mightiest knights on life as the stories said.

Determination had not been enough. Armed might had spared but two of them. Caution had not saved them. After a night spent searching, then hiding and fighting, followed by most of a day of running, Constans was feeling as cautious as he ever had, and still he couldn't quite believe they had gotten this far.

Although it shimmered in the heat, the edge of the valley was there. So close. A scramble up the jagged rock edges and they would be within yards of the camp. Squire Brody, who had been left to guard it. The river, so cool and blue. *The horses.*

"Come," he said again, and lurched forward.

An hour's painful, stumbling slog got them within steps of the ridge.

"Did you hear that?" asked Sir Infaustus.

Together they stopped and stood with heads cocked. Sir Constans squinted, trying to see through his doubling vision and behind the boulders that surrounded them. Nothing moved.

But there it was. A slithery, scraping noise. Too close.

Without a word he grasped Infaustus's upper arm again and pulled. Infaustus had to hop and limp his way along and would have fallen without that hold. They jerked towards the ridge, poised above them like a frozen obsidian wave.

He had to let go of his companion as they threw themselves at the boulders. An explosion of rattles and slithering behind them lent urgency to his feet.

Unyielding rock dug into his stomach. He used his forearms and kicked with his legs to haul himself forward, like the biggest, oldest frog in a burned black pond. This undignified scramble didn't matter. Up, and onward, was everything important in the world.

Beside him the breastplate clanged and scraped as Infaustus was yanked backwards. He gave one hoarse scream as he thudded to the dirt below.

"Brody!" Constans roared. There was a chance they were close enough to camp for the squire to hear. He fumbled at the hilt of his sword. "Brody!"

Sir Infaustus was already twitching his last when Constans turned. A stinger withdrew from the back of his fellow knight's neck, glittering and shivering.

The Princess had found them.

She looked exactly as she had in the castle when Constans saw her last. Her pale, flawless skin was nearly luminous in sunlight. Golden hair flowed down around her, set off by the iridescent green-blue of her dress. The lovely locks brushed Infaustus's still body with gently curling tendrils. Sharp, almost reptilian, the features of her face matched the jagged edges of the glass rock around them.

And, exactly as he had seen before, the dead knight at her feet had lost his own features as his face blurred under the sheath of her venom. The clear, sticky strings would spread, wrapping and binding. Infaustus would become nothing more than her seventeenth meal, hanging in the Great Hall like the others. Little cocooned pigwiggins, waiting to be served up for tea.

There was nothing Constans could do for him. There might not be anything he could do for himself.

"Squire Brody!" he begged, in a last, desperate shout. As he had suspected, the sword was useless in his trembling hand so he let it drop and turned to climb again.

His fingers bit into the rock. His feet dug for purchase.

Fingers like chilled iron wrapped around his ankle. Before he could try to twist away, he'd already landed on his stomach. His chin bounced on the ground and his teeth clacked together. Breath whooshed out of him, sending up a puff of dust.

*:Is this your Squire Brody:*

The thought appeared softly in his mind, along with an image. Gangly limbs and a shock of red hair. Freckles and wide, frightened, green-hazel eyes.

"That's Brody," he coughed. *Can she not speak? I suppose not, with the poison sacs.* He dragged himself closer to where the sword had dropped. Cuts and gashes had little effect on this creature, whatever she was, but he had to try.

Her hand seemed to freeze his ankle, so cold was it. His heart hammered inside him, urging him on. With one huge lunge he grasped the hilt.

:*He has been my guest these past two days:*

This thought came to him with slight overtones of satisfaction. He snarled and whirled around, sinking the edge of the sword into her fragile ankle, just above the blue satin slipper.

She shook her head, reached down, and tugged the sword out. Clear ichor flowed from the wound, the same in appearance to her venom. It slowed and stopped almost immediately, as it had every other time one of the knights had managed to strike her.

:*He tasted delicious*: she thought to Sir Constans.

"He was only a boy. Damn you!" he said.

:*This has been done, already. Your wishes will not add to my damning:*

His weight seemed to give her no trouble as she tugged him over to lie beside Infaustus. Constans twisted and fought, trying to drag his ankle away from her implacable grip or catch a rock to hold onto. Finally, he threw handfuls of grit and pebbles, coating the skirts of her pretty dress with dusty black. None of it halted his forward movement. He stopped when a flailing hand brushed the sticky body of his comrade.

She flipped him over neatly and put a hand to his chest, leaning on him to hold him still.

He hadn't seen her eyes before, in the castle. He'd been too far away. Instead of the blue or blue-green he would have expected, they were red. Deep, heart's-blood red, from edge to edge, unrelieved by pupil or iris.

Her mouth opened, pursing as if she were considering a complicated question. He shuddered and closed his eyes.

Venom dripped onto his leg, soft as the touch of new snow. The cold was immediate, spreading and numbing on his aching muscles. If he hadn't already known what that feeling meant it would have been a blessing on this airless, heated sand.

His eyes flew open. "Are you not going to kill me?"

*:My larder is full, and I am lonely. I require your company for some days.:*

"Well, you can't have it. Stick me with your damned pointer, as you did the others. And have done."

*:I will enjoy speaking with you, old man. You amuse me:*

Smiling slightly, she bent to the cocoon that was Sir Infaustus. He closed his eyes again, rather than watch the venom string out of that rosebud pink mouth. His stomach heaved.

When he heard the slithering rustle of movement, he looked. A long, thick string stretched between Infaustus and her hand like a lead.

Cold spread from his calf to his thigh, leaving blank nothing behind. Already filaments of it crept over to touch his other leg. They were being bound together. His heart thrashed, the rhythm strange.

She carried him over her small shoulder so that his face thumped into the smooth satin covering her back. If he lifted his head he could see the body of his friend, bumping along behind them. So he kept his head lowered.

*All these years*, Constans thought. *All the knights that went to rescue the Princess in the Tower.* His head was pounding. Every thought clanged against the inside of his skull. That insidious numbness had started to take hold of his other calf.

*And no one ever thought to ask* why *she should be locked up in this godforsaken waste in the first place.*


**S.E. White** is an author, bookstagram addict, and blogger. Her articles can be found on various websites like Books Rock My World. Her short story "Dinner is Better When We Eat Together" won an honorable mention in the 2018 Writer's Digest competition. "The Princess In The Tower" is the first short story of hers to appear in a collection.

## Slay a Fledgling
## by Elyssa Campbell

Staring up at what remained of the walls, Lucien knew fay monsters had destroyed the town.

Not by the sheer savagery of how they had torn through—humans were capable of such blind wickedness and industrial weapons could inflict damage of that magnitude. However, invading armies did not carry off the dead. Whoever, *whatever* had attacked this village and the still-smoking manor house up the hill had left no bodies lying among the blood and rubble. Lucien's dark bay mare tossed her head at the sharp scent.

*"Je sais, ma belle,"* Lucien cooed, stroking her neck.

Behind, one of Lucien's men stumbled down from his horse and retched into the brush. No one teased him.

*"Capitaine!"* Lucien's Lieutenant Morin came riding down the street at a brisk pace, then dismounted and led his horse through the rubble of the wall. "I scouted the town. There is no trail, but a breach in the north-eastern wall points towards the village of Patelin, God protect them."

"Did you find survivors?" Lucien asked.

Morin removed his tricorne and shook his balding head solemnly. Morin was old enough to be Lucien's father, but no one doubted the *Comte Lucien de Cousteau*'s command. The king was the godfather of Lucien's infant son. As well as his royal connection, Lucien had been blessed with an intelligent mind and the charisma of a natural leader.

Lucien looked around at his men's weary faces and battered navy uniforms. Defeat weighed them down each time they came upon a ruined town.

More fay monsters crossed the Frozenfinger Mountains into the realms of men every year, reviving superstition in the border towns, snuffing out reason and enlightenment. City-folk had scoffed at the rumors until a troupe of farmers had laid a dead manticore at the King of Sadvrenne's feet. Lucien—fascinated by the pale, twisted corpse while the painted court had gasped and shrank—had volunteered. He'd since volunteered for every mission to exterminate the fay terrorizing the north.

Their current quest was the most dangerous yet. The king wouldn't have let Lucien go, but it was the most alive he'd seen his beloved friend in months.

"This town was destroyed a few days ago. We are closing in— the horde appears to be ranging over this area." Lucien spun his horse and rode over to the sick soldier who was now sitting by the side of the dirt road. He reached down to offer his hand. He helped the soldier to his feet. "Up on your horse, man." Lucien's dark eyes were steel, but empathy laced his voice. "We will not fail *sa Majesté* and our brothers and sisters in the north."

The rocky, winding road smelled of rain. In the distance, the jagged peaks of the Frozenfinger Mountains emerged from the fog, pointing towards the faintly visible twin moons.

The Frozenfingers were swords that guarded the western human kingdoms against the uncharted fay east—from the monsters, fay people, and magic that had once terrorized the whole world. The mountains had protected Sadvrenne for centuries, but no longer, it seemed. Lucien kept his gaze on the mountains, a gaze that asked, *if you are truly failing us, then what will be humanity's fate?*

The early spring landscape stretched all around: rolling hills and budding woods filled with bright birdsong. Life and mirth returned to Lucien's men. They gossiped, swore, and laughed raucously. They teased one another about their families, about sexual prowess or lack thereof. To alarm a newly betrothed youth, Morin began to recount a merry warning of the birth of his oldest child, exaggerating his helpless panic… then someone cleared his throat, and Morin stopped, ashamed. Tension hung in the air. It took a moment for Lucien to notice, and only then did Morin's benign story begin to weigh on him, reminding him of the birth of his own son. Lucien pulled his tricorne lower over his forehead.

The newly betrothed soldier called up to Lucien, "My Lord, is it true that the king is going to marry a fay?"

Morin scoffed before Lucien could answer: "Where have you been, lad? Yes, he is going to marry a beautiful lady of the fair-folk."

"I've heard tales about the age of fay," said the young soldier with confidence. "Why would *sa Majesté* do such a thing?"

Lucien silently agreed. The king had returned from a tour of the north enthralled with a mysterious fay lady. Lucien had spent many futile hours trying to change his best friend's mind, reminding him that the fair-folk were as different from men as housecats from tigers, as dogs from wolves.

"Can't you hear?" Morin said. "A *very beautiful*, exotic lady whose lineage might go back to the age of fay and the fay empire? Our king is already divine in the eyes of the people. This will make his heir a deity in the neighboring kingdoms and the eyes of history."

"Deity? More like a demon whose ancestors once ruled over men," another scoffed. "We're hunting fay. Now the king wants to marry one?"

"You misunderstand what the fay people are, men," Lucien called back in a half-hearted defense of his king's decision. Even if he disagreed, he would never criticize the king publicly. "The fair-folk are not fay monsters, just as men are not beasts."

#

Wild fields became tilled farmland. The road sloped gently as they neared the forested foothills of the Frozenfingers. Fog settled into the folds of the valley, obscuring the village which was tucked like a bird's nest in the center: Patelin.

212

The air was quiet. Lucien realized that the birds had stopped singing.

"It doesn't look like there was any trouble here," Morin said, catching up to Lucien. "Are you certain we're still within the horde's hunting grounds?"

Lucien held up a closed fist to stop his men and leaned forward on his horse, eyes narrowing, listening. A lonely breeze blew through Lucien's dark hair. The horses fidgeted uneasily.

A hazy shadow, formless in the low-hanging clouds, swooped over the dozen cottages. An alarm bell cut through the silence, followed by faint, rising screams and the blast of musket rifles. The shadow reappeared larger than before, dipped into the village, then soared upwards on mighty wings and disappeared in the thick clouds.

Morin breathed, his big brown eyes wide, "God save us, is that..."

A shriek echoed across the valley—a sound like nothing Lucien had ever heard—like the grinding roar of a breaking train and thunder. It reverberated in the hollow chasm of his chest. The horses spooked. The men cried out as they attempted to regain control.

*A wyvern.* Lucien had vastly underestimated the threat. They weren't tracking a fay horde. They were following a single monster, one that had not been seen in the human kingdoms for millennia. Their weapons would be useless.

Lucien spun his horse and trotted back to his men. They were staring wide-eyed at the clouded sky, blinded by fear. He pointed towards the village. "Those people are defenseless!" he shouted. "We're their only hope."

A soldier at the back of the company removed the long rifle strapped across his back. He hoisted it to the sky in one hand. "We'll kill that monster for you, *Capitaine*!"

Lucien shook his head. "We'll need ballistae and steel bolts to kill that thing. I need two men to carry the message to the king: send a small army north on the railroad." Lucien selected two of his fastest riders. "Ride back to the nearest train station and inform *sa Majesté* of the threat. I'm sure you understand that speed is of the essence."

"Yes, my Lord!"

"We'll get it done, sir."

With quick salutes, they spun their horses and rode back the way the company had come.

Lucien rode up to Morin. "For now, we have to get those people to safety."

"How?" Morin asked. "There's no shelter for miles! They'll be picked off like field mice."

The shadow descended upon the town once more, then swooped up, followed by echoing blasts of gunfire. The grim truth of Morin's words sunk in as Lucien surveyed the landscape. Kilometers of exposed farmland ended in forests that the wyvern could tear through like a barley field.

Lucien's face was set. "Then we must make it lose interest in the village." He raised his eyes to the mountain peaks. "I'll lead it toward the fingers."

"Not alone, my Lord," Morin said.

Lucien could feel the weight of the older man's gaze. Morin knew it would be a suicide mission.

"No." Lucien shook his head. "You'll lead the others in protecting the village."

"Sir, let me go."

"I have nothing left to lose." The comment escaped Lucien's lips without thought.

"You have a boy, my Lord!" Morin shouted at the side of Lucien's face, prepared to knock some sense into his captain. "Do you think that your Lady wife would have wanted him to grow up without a father?"

Shame settled on Lucien's shoulders. He turned to his men. "The Lieutenant and I will need extra ammunition." He gestured to the nearest soldier. "Hand me your rifle." The soldier hesitantly handed over the gun. Lucien loaded it with multiple rounds and tucked extra cartridges into his saddlebag. "The rest of you protect the civilians!"

They galloped into the chaos of Patelin. People ran to-and-fro. One house had been torn apart, leaving wreckage strewn across the road. The lonely bell in the chapel clanged a futile alarm. Lucien spotted a brave, foolish boy in the middle of the street. The boy pointed an old-fashioned muzzle-loading rifle to the sky, watching for a shadow in the clouds.

Lucien dismounted. He ran over and grabbed the boy by the arm. "*Arrête*! You'll only enrage it. Get your family and go hide in your cellar."

The boy looked up at Lucien, his coiling hair drenched with sweat. For a fear-stricken moment, he seemed not to understand, then he ran off to spread the word. Lucien saw his men fanning out through the village, searching for survivors, barking orders.

"*Capitaine*!" Morin stopped his horse next to Lucien and pointed to the sky.

Shielding his eyes, Lucien glimpsed a black shape against the overcast sun. With a deafening shriek that shook the earth, a colorless terror descended below the clouds and dove into the village: six entirely black eyes and translucent, leathery wings as large as battleship sails. His ears ringing, Lucien aimed, fired. His shot glanced off the wyvern's scales like the steel side of a steam engine. The wyvern grabbed an ox between razor-sharp claws and, flapping its wings with the force of a gale, took off. Lucien reloaded, shot again.

The shot hit the side of the wyvern's head, a hairsbreadth from one of its black eyes.

Lucien had its attention now.

Dropping its prey, the wyvern turned back with a blood-curdling shriek and dove. Lucien slung his rifle over his shoulder, ran back to his mare, and swung into the saddle. They took off through the village. Behind, he heard Morin fire.

They galloped across the farmland towards the towering mountain range. Lucien felt the pounding wind of the wyvern's wings. He heard his horse panting from the effort and terror of outrunning death.

Every second was drawn out in a line stretching to eternity, measured by the furious gallop of hooves, fractured by Morin's futile attempts to draw the wyvern away from Lucien—shots from horseback, each one missing its flying target.

The world jolted as Lucien's horse stumbled over a patch of soft earth. Lucien's foot caught in the stirrup as they fell. He cried out in shock and agony as fire shot up his leg into his hip, then his head hit the dirt. His ears rang; the grey sky swam. Lucien was pinned to the earth, his mare was struggling to get up, screaming. A blurry form dove toward him.

As Lucien saw the wyvern skimming the ground, his sharpest thought was that he'd lost his hat.

A horse and rider ran between him and the wyvern. Lucien shouted in helpless despair as the wyvern grabbed Morin and his mount in its two massive, razor-sharp feet, then flapped its mighty wings and lifted off. Lucien stretched, fumbling for a rifle that lay just out of reach. Pain shot up his leg. He gritted his teeth. Grasping the butt of the gun in his fingertips, Lucien pulled it into his arms. He dug ammunition from his saddlebag and started firing half-blind shot.

The wyvern dropped Morin.

Horse and rider fell from such a height that Lucien knew both had been killed. The wyvern spread its wings and turned back. Lucien smelled death on the wind as it approached. The wyvern bared its teeth, but skimmed above Lucien and grabbed him with its feet. Blinding pain flashed in his vision, one of its talons pierced his military jacket. It pulled him from beneath his horse, into the sky, toward the mountains.

Trees raced below. Lucien raised his head and admired the monster carrying him toward certain death—the might of its shoulders, the white feathers of its neck, and the armored scales of its belly.

Lucien prayed that his men had cleared the village, and that word would reach the king.

#

A faint whistle turned the wyvern's head.

The wyvern responded in kind, mimicking the sound. It spiraled toward the forested mountainside. Lucien covered his face as branches flew up, breaking like twigs. It dropped him. He hit the earth with a yelp and rolled to a stop.

Flapping its wings, the wyvern landed in a nearby clearing.

Lucien hastily propped himself up on his good arm and watched the wyvern. It began to clean itself, combing through its feathers with its teeth. Confusion surged through Lucien's gut; why had the monster forgotten him?

A gunshot sent cawing crows flying into the sky. The wyvern breathed a pitiful whine, then collapsed.

The bullet had passed straight through one of the wyvern's six black eyes. Lucien kept himself flat to the ground. He scanned his wooded surroundings for the sharpshooter. In the dappled sun and shadow filtering through the scattered trees, Lucien glimpsed what looked like an angel astride a white horse. It dismounted and approached.

Cold apprehension surged through Lucien. It was not an angel. It was a demon—a fay woman in a long travelling cloak clutching a hunting rifle.

Fighting the pain in his hip, Lucien climbed to his feet with the help of a thick poplar tree trunk, putting all his weight on his good leg.

Lucien regarded his unexpected savior through sweat-drenched hair clinging to his brow. She was a terrible beauty. The first thing Lucien noticed was her eyes; her coldly brilliant black eyes looked like two deep holes set in her face that devoured the surrounding daylight. A mound of colorless hair was braided back behind pointed ears. Her skin was translucent, paper-thin over black veins. She looked a hundred years old or nineteen.

"Quid tibi… nomen est—what is the name for you?" Lucien asked roughly in the language of the first men to come to this world—the last language men and fay had in common.

The faintest suggestion of a smile parted her pale lips but did not reach her dreadful eyes. It was the implied smile of an instructor about to correct an ignorant student. "You may call me Marcielle," she said flatly in Lucien's native tongue—one that had evolved ages after men and fair-folk had gone their separate ways.

"That is a Sadvrenne name."

Tilting her neck, Marcielle slipped the strap of her rifle over her head, so the gun hung across her back. "It is."

"But you are not…" Lucien trailed off.

Marcielle's wholly black gaze dragged past him to the dead wyvern. Wordlessly, she dropped her horse's reins and walked over to the massive corpse. Lucien couldn't read her face, whether she felt triumph at having felled the monster, regret at having killed a fellow fay creature, or nothing. She had saved his life, but Lucien knew it would be wise to be wary of this fay stranger.

"Is it dead?" Lucien asked.

Marcielle made a small noise of affirmation. "You are fortunate. She was taking you to feed her young."

Lucien laughed despite himself. He slid back to the forest floor, clutching his upper left leg. The fiery pain was coming from a dislocated hip and injured femur. Whether the bone was broken, Lucien could only guess.

"It only left town to follow you because you were headed towards its nest. I spotted it about a kilometer into the mountains." Marcielle pointed a leather-gloved hand toward the jagged peaks of the Frozenfingers. Her voice echoed with a distant, scientific curiosity. "How long have fay monsters been in your country? Months? Years?"

"Years. If there is a nest, as you say, we must destroy it."

Marcielle turned, looking him up and down. "You're injured," she said as if noticing for the first time. Her face set with the focused intensity of a nurse, she came over and examined him. She pulled away shreds of navy fabric to reveal an ugly gash between his collarbone and right shoulder. Without a moment's warning, she turned her attention to his leg and set his hip back in place.

"*Aïe*," Lucien yelped.

Marcielle released his leg, then went around to his good side and helped him to his feet. She was quite strong for her size. The smell of her hair brushed faintly over him—rain, earth and fading perfume. "The damage to your shoulder seems to be superficial, but you may never walk or ride properly again unless you receive medical care." She whistled, and her horse trotted over through the underbrush. "Take my horse back to town."

Lucien supported himself with a hand on the pommel. He tried and failed to climb up. "Forgive me, *mademoiselle*, but I must see that nest. Fay nests are still rare on this side of the Frozenfingers, but the terrors of the east are spreading westward. We must—" he tried again, then almost lost his footing, "—know what is coming."

Marcielle watched him, unblinking. "I will not help you destroy yourself, *Capitaine de Cousteau*."

Lucien had to admire her face. It was an extraordinary, intelligent face, and watching her think was like watching a pair of songbirds fight. Clenching his jaw, Lucien summoned the determination to hoist himself into the saddle. "So, you know who I am."

Marcielle must have decided that his resolve would outlast her patience because she took the reins from Lucien and began to lead them up the mountainside.

#

"I am not here by chance," Marcielle admitted once they had been climbing for several minutes. "I was sent to help with the king's permission."

"What interest does your king have among men?" Lucien asked warily.

"Your king is my king." Marcielle picked their way through the scant underbrush. "He told me of your campaign a few days after you'd left. I knew that you were dealing with a wyvern. I took the train north, then tracked the nest directly rather than following the wyvern's trail of destruction."

Lucien stared down at her white head. He remembered the hours his best friend had raved, spellbound, about his magnificent bride-to-be… and the hours Lucien had spent trying to change his mind. What were the odds that a fay acquainted with the King of Sadvrenne was other than the phenomenon the king was going to marry?

"My apologies, my Lady. Are you the king's betrothed?"

Marcielle kept facing forward, but Lucien glimpsed the ghost of a smile that was marred by her wholly black eyes. "A fair deduction, *Capitaine*, but not I. My elder sister will marry the king. I have merely been graced with land and titles befitting of a queen's sister."

"Why send a Lady to track down a wyvern?"

"Which one of us managed to slay the monster?" she replied.

Lucien laughed out loud, then regretted it as pain shot through the gash in his shoulder. *Fair enough*, he smiled inwardly. "So, there must be more of your kind left than we had imagined."

"If you believed us to be extinct, then I am sorry to disappoint you." Marcielle's tone was faintly condescending, or perhaps remorseful, or both. Lucien listened, curious, and unoffended. "The east is bigger than you can imagine. It is the whole world, and you menfolk live only at the edge of it."

"Our legends say that this whole world once belonged to you, and that mankind crossed over from another." Lucien waited, but Marcielle didn't comment. "How about magic? Does that still exist in the east?"

"Magic is starving, and it wants to take the whole world with it. The fair-folk killed my brother for it." Marcielle turned her face up to him. Her white lashes blinked slowly—white-winged moths. "Why am I sharing this with you?"

"I'm sorry," Lucien said sincerely.

Marcielle nodded curtly, gratefully.

#

The forest thinned as Marcielle climbed, leading Lucien on horseback. Patches of melting snow clung to the shade of stunted pine trees and sparse bushes. The rocky terrain curved and flattened. Fighting to ignore the dull pain in his hip and shoulder, Lucien imagined that they had come across the remains of an ancient mountain road. He pondered how many strangers, human and fay, had passed this way over the ages.

They came upon a large cave in the exposed stone side of an outcrop. It looked like a dark, gaping wound in the rock. Lucien covered his nose and mouth as a gust of wind carried the scent of the cave. It reeked like animal—rot, decay, and old blood.

Marcielle dropped the reins and stalked toward the entrance. She listened, then gestured for him to come.

"Is this the nest?" Lucien stumbled from the saddle.

With a quick nod, Marcielle slung off her rifle and handed it to him. Lucien checked it for rounds then followed her inside the cave.

The smell was overwhelming, even in the cool air. Darkness pressed on Lucien's eyes. It took a moment for them to adjust, and when they did, Marcielle was crouching at the side of a nest the size of a small corral. Small sounds similar to birdsong echoed off the rock. In the middle of the nest, two shapes squirmed among scattered bones. *Are those…*

"Fledgling wyverns," Marcielle answered before Lucien could voice his thought. Light as a cat on her feet, she slunk across the nest and lifted one into her arms. It flapped paper-thin wings but stilled when she whistled to it softly. Such a wonderous smile broke across Marcielle's face that Lucien forgot, momentarily, about the haunting effect of her eyes. She gestured with her chin for him to join her.

Lucien set the rifle on the ground. He approached with a supporting hand on the wall, then stopped just behind her. *"C'est magnifique."*

It was no bigger than a fox and covered in dull grey plumage. It flexed its lacelike wings, docile in Marcielle's arms.

"It does not fear your touch."

In response, Marcielle whistled again, and the wyvern responded in kind: It made a soft, melodic cooing noise. Lucien realized the echoes of birdsong came from the fledglings, and that Marcielle had called the full-grown wyvern to the ground.

The fledgling lunged for a stray piece of Marcielle's hair. She yelped in surprise while Lucien let out a snort of laughter. "Would you—" she craned her neck to try to keep her head out of reach of its snapping jaws "—like to hold him?"

"It looks dangerous," Lucien grinned.

"Very funny," she shot back.

Lucien let her place the fledgling in his arms. It settled against his chest, heavier than he'd expected, yet surprisingly soft to the touch. Awe tingled; he was holding a wyvern. Three pairs of double-lidded black eyes opened and blinked eerily at him. He saw something in its eyes that he did not expect to see in the eyes of a monster, something much like personhood. The wyvern was conscious that it was a being, that he was a separate being… "It is intelligent," Lucien realized.

"Indeed. That's why they are so dangerous." Marcielle said it matter-of-factly as if she had known many monsters that were more than beasts.

"It is so defenseless. Where is its armor?"

"Scales will grow on his sides and underbelly as he ages. These fledglings might be the last of their kind." Marcielle took off a leather glove and brushed her delicate fingers over its head, between the two nubs of its emerging horns. "That makes what we have to do all the more unfortunate."

#

Marcielle said it with the distant interest he had heard from her before, yet this time it seemed out of place. Lucien looked at the beautiful monster he held. He had briefly forgotten about their purpose here.

Lucien considered whether a world without fay would be a better world or a lesser one. Lucien raised his eyes from the monster in his arms to the fay lady who stood before him, and he found the answer. "We are Sadvrenne are a modern people. It seems a terrible thing to exterminate an entire species out of fear. Should we destroy tigers or wolves simply because they are dangerous?"

"Hand him over, *Capitaine*. I will take care of it."

"I know a circus man in the south of Sadvrenne who collects fay monsters. Let's take these to him." Lucien searched her expression for signs of weakness. "Wouldn't it be wonderful for men of science to study the durability of its scales, and adapt it to our armor? For Sadvrenne children to grow up and be inspired by the sight of this creature."

For a brief moment, Lucien believed that he'd found a chink in her armor, then a wall of indifference passed over her face. "That's a wonderful thought, but not reasonable. Fay have no place in the lands of men."

"I disagree. People would come from all around to see this wyvern. I would take my son to see it." Lucien gazed unflinchingly into her wholly black eyes. "I want my son to meet you, too."

"To meet me." Marcielle's pale brows furrowed in genuine disbelief. "Whatever for?"

Lucien was pleased to see that she was caught off guard. Without skipping a beat, he said, "I understand why my dear king fell in love with your sister."

Lucien thought it was checkmate; he was sorely mistaken. A smile twisted one corner of Marcielle's lips and lit her black eyes with an eerie light. The sight made Lucien's skin crawl; it was the same dread he'd felt as a boy when bishops warned of demons. She whispered something unintelligible in two layered, unearthly voices, and the creature in Lucien's arms simply, soundlessly died. It was magic—but not as he'd imagined it. No spectacle, no spells or witchcraft, just a quiet wish fulfilled by a horrible, untamed power.

Lucien dropped the wyvern and stared, dumbfounded, at its corpse.

"Look at me, *Capitaine*, and see why my kind still has no place among yours. It's because of magic." Visceral disgust contorted her voice. "All fay are infected, but I am one of the few who can still use it."

Lucien raised his gaze to her face. "My men were right; you and your sister are a threat to the king." Backing unsteadily out of the nest, his heel bumped the rifle. He picked it up. "You're no different from the wyverns and the other fay monsters that terrorize us—a plague upon our land." Lucien cocked the rifle and pointed it at her. Reason told him to uphold the oath he'd sworn to king and country, but Lucien had no desire to pull the trigger. "Raise your hands, fay, and step out into the sun."

Wordlessly, Marcielle complied. Unstable on his feet, but not lowering the hunting rifle, Lucien escorted her out of the cave. The sunlight blinded him, but fresh air was a relief after the palpable decay inside the den. The wind had banished all trace of the morning's fog. It blew through the free strands escaping Marcielle's braided hair.

Marcielle wandered to the edge of the outcrop, overlooking the forested valley. "Whatever you believe about me, I want you to know that my sister is no threat to the king." She turned, pain flashing briefly in her wholly black eyes before she was able to guard her heart. "The king loves her because of who she is—beautiful and kind—nothing more, not for some political scheme or because she has a spell over him. In fact, she has no control of magic."

"But *you* do." Lucien extracted what she had not said. "*Sa Majesté* didn't fall for her on the tour of the north by chance, did he?"

Marcielle approached in deadly silence, stopping so close that she had to look up into Lucien's gaze. Lucien was already lowering the rifle when she grabbed the barrel and pointed it away from her person. "Only a human ruler could protect her from the fay. Our high birth did not protect my family from being hunted by our own kind because of *my* ability."

"You're refugees," Lucien realized. "Just like that wyvern and her offspring."

Marcielle curled both hands around the rifle. "Give this back if you're too cowardly to kill the other fledgling. The only way to stop a deadly plague is to burn every infected thing."

Lucien decided not to let her have it, even if it became a tug-of-war. A wry smile crinkled the corners of his eyes. "*Every* infected thing—like yourself?"

Marcielle's slender frame slumped ever so slightly. She let go.

"You would destroy yourself?" Lucien's voice was dangerously soft. "You fled the east to save your life and your sister's. Yet you suggest that I should kill you, here and now, to protect my people from magic. Your philosophy is a contradiction, my Lady."

Marcielle rounded on him, a flash of anger contorting her delicate face. "Do not speak to me of hypocrisy. *You* have a son yet relentlessly pursue self-destruction!"

Marcielle peeled her glare from him and turned back to the cave. Satisfied at having produced an emotional response in her, Lucien was slow to realize that Marcielle still intended to kill the other wyvern. She would kill it with or without the gun—with magic—and in doing so, perhaps kill something inside herself. Lucien dropped the gun. He lunged and seized her arm. He ignored the dull pain in his hip as it bore his weight. "You're better than this."

"Wrong. This is what I am." Marcielle yanked her arm with inhuman strength. Lucien held on but lost his footing and dragged her with him. She let out a cry of surprise as they tumbled together down the steep slope of the mountain.

Fire shot through his shoulder and hip as he dislodged rocks and earth, rolling to a stop against a shrub on the outcrop below. He turned onto his back and stared at the spinning sky. He let out a string of curses that turned into a bout of helpless laughter.

He watched, dazed, as Marcielle's blurry shape approached.

"Your idealism is madness!" Disheveled hair stuck to the breathless face that stared down at him. He followed her outstretched gesture toward what he assumed was the wyvern cave. It was indistinguishable from the rest of the rocky mountainside. "Soon that monster will be a terror just like her mother. You saw the bones littering the cave."

Lucien memorized the way sunlight refracted across her face, an artist appreciating a timeless statue.

"You must harden your heart, *Capitaine*, or you will never be able to protect what you love—why are you laughing?"

Lucien's laughter softened into a small smile. He was beginning to understand Marcielle: her fears, the contradictions within her heart driving her futile attempts at atonement. She was reasonable, but reasonable was wrong. "No."

"No?"

"No," Lucien repeated simply and watched her expression soften.

No, Lucien would not do the reasonable thing. No, he would not protect his king and country at the expense of Marcielle and the fledgling. His smile broke. He lay on the dirt and wept. The emotion Lucien had withheld since the death of his wife poured out, the sorrow of losing the light of his life, the terror of being a father in a world where wickedness reigned. Lucien would dare to let the pain go and love again.

"Help me stand," Lucien said. Wordlessly, Marcielle took his good arm and helped him to his feet.

A melodic cry that rose into a shriek echoed over the rocky mountainside. Their heads turned to the sky in shock. Lucien wiped his eyes with the sleeve of his army jacket. The fledgling wyvern had taken flight; shakily at first, then it spiraled and soared toward the horizon.

For a moment of innocent wonder, they held one another,

savoring the wyvern's beauty.

**Elyssa Campbell** is an education student at Trinity Western University in Canada. Her fantasy fiction appeared in *The Showbear Family Circus* and has been accepted for an upcoming issue of *Bards and Sages Quarterly*.

# The Overlander's Poison
## by Amy de la Force

Nancy West shifted the hay bale from her shoulder to the stockpile, the overripe scent of straw carried on a bulldust breeze. Blue and white chequered shirt knotted at the waist, her rolled sleeves were scuffed with terracotta dirt; casualties of the plan she was cultivating like the mole (wombat) she was.

Because Nancy was a plant. A vampire hunter prowling across the Australian outback, she'd ridden into Tima Cattle Station days ago posing as the new farm–girl next door. And the tiny town was talking, which was perfect. Now all she needed was for the grapevine to wend its way to wherever her bloodsucking target was hiding.

Nancy fished a pink compact from her jeans and clicked it open. Embedding at Tima had been easy, with her sun-streaked hair and freckles sprinkled down her nose, which crinkled when she grinned; the good-looking new girl. She rarely wore make-up, but for jobs like this one, she turned up the girly-factor with lip gloss, blush and highlighter — the highlighter a defensive aid, based with vampire-incapacitating gold. Taking a brush to the shimmery powder, she swept it along her neck, collarbone, the insides of her wrists and elbows, and anywhere major arteries lay exposed. She knew it was only a matter of time before she drew out the vamp, so day after day, Nancy bided her night-time.

She didn't have to wait long.

Nancy angled an ear to the outfields, alone with the drowsy lowing of the cows. It wouldn't be long until that syrupy sunset faded to a cold, hard black, and with it, every semblance of her artful disguise.

Because Nancy wasn't a fledgling 'jillaroo' station hand. And as she strapped her shotgun to her back, revolver to her thigh and concealed her knife, she couldn't help but grin at the thought. With a final check of her weapons, she resumed the default left-to-right sweep of her environment and limbered up. There was a word for what she was — a member of the clandestine vampire hunting mercenaries of Australia. Hailing from a sordid past, when a prison colony had landed on these shores, and ignorance had stowed then unleashed the undead horrors of their motherland. A single word, with singular purpose: to kill all vampires. Her oath, the day everything had changed.

The day she'd sworn she would never again kneel helpless before death.

*Overlander.*

Tima Station had called. And so Nancy had come.

She got to work.

As the outback slumbered under the sky's kaleidoscope of stars, Nancy could almost forget she was hunting the undead. Spinifex was cast in starlight and the promise of a waxing moon, the landscape dip-dyed in ethereal blacks and greys and whites. Too much white, Nancy cursed in silence. But visibility was the point — as uncomfortably exposed as she felt out in the open, it's what her damsel ruse required.

Nancy executed the last step of her trap with absolute precision, slicing her forearm and smearing the blood every few tree trunks or so from the north-western paddock out into the underbrush, leaving a gory breadcrumb trail. The scent of her blood would continue past a loose line of shrubs to the tree where she currently lay in wait. Nancy patched her forearm, flexing her fingers. It was a solid plan.

Especially considering the anti-vampire landmine — packed with gold, sun-metal of the ancients — buried as the crow flies between her last blood smear and where she stood nursing her 12 gauge shotgun.

Soon enough, she had company… Twin greenish-grey orbs, like an animal's eyes but wrong somehow, materialised in the darkness. Dead ahead.

The vampire, someone in his day, judging by the frayed yet tailored suit, edged from the shadows into the moon's sliver of a beam. Only… Nancy's grey eyes narrowed, marking the sallow skin, the off-kilter movements, the sheer starvation in his face. Alarm roiled in her gut. This deathbed vamp — he'd had more than enough time to divide and devour the herd, hell, the whole damn station. *What was going on?*

And she hadn't questioned it, Nancy realised. Her callout, the assignment: kill the vampire slaughtering the station's herd, a classic tactic to petrify human prey. Grisly scenes; cattle decapitated, limbs ripped then playfully arranged in macabre motifs. The metallic spice of blood-soaked meat had threatened even Nancy's seasoned stomach. She'd upped the prey ante with a bleeding young female separated from her herd — herself, right now. But the fact was, there hadn't been a single human casualty. And she hadn't questioned it. As the weight of her undue diligence pressed upon her, the vampire turned and hell-born pupils met her own. Before she could open her mouth, the *click* of her explosive armed. She watched the vampire's gaze flutter to his feet, then to Nancy. There was something, a sorrow, to his stare-

"Trap…" The vampire whispered, the desiccated sound showing he hadn't spoken, fed, in days, maybe weeks. Before she could stop him, he lifted his foot — and exploded into a million bloody chunks, metal and flesh raining down where Nancy stood rooted to the smoking ground, the blast rending the darkness.

"Woah-ho-*ho!*" An astonished laugh, followed by raucous claps, sounded from behind the ill-fated shrubs. "I know Overlanders are an enterprising bunch, but that was *impressive!*" Nancy dropped into a crouch, back against a paper-bark gum, and glanced in the direction of the newcomer. Clocking the telltale sheen of undead pupils, she whipped her shotgun to her chest before zagging to the next tree, boots hushing the clay beneath her feet.

Nancy didn't hesitate and emptied twin gold rounds at the second vampire, body flowing with the kick and boom of her shotgun. This one was clearly not starving and moved inhumanly fast. Gritting her teeth, she fired again, this time catching him in the chest — centimetres from the heart and with an exit wound. *Dammit!* The fleeting kiss of gold wouldn't be enough. He laboured towards her, smiling, blood black on the dirt, as Nancy flicked her revolver from her holster. And aimed it squarely at his head. "Take another step," she said, the challenge laced with keen contempt.

"Okay — you got me." The vampire's gaze lowered to his blazer lapel. "And the Zegna," he said, raising an eyebrow. The overhanging crescent moon revealed a slender figure, not unlike the first vamp. Nancy lasered in on the expensive watch and shoes, the clean lines of his clothing, and that hair — city-slick. No one sustained that level of polish, not out here. *What, and who, the hell…*

"Answers." Nancy barked. "What's your game? Why the decoy?" She fired her gun into his kneecap. Another clean wound, though the vampire's wince was gratifying. "Assuming you're fed, that'll take five minutes to heal. Talk!"

The vampire's expression was a half-smirk. "Come now, *Nancy*," he said, and she stiffened at the recognition. "What else does one do so far from civilisation? I've simply been having a little fun… Torturing livestock, backpackers — the same thing, really — while I waited for a new Overlander to arrive." He shook his head, *tsk*-ing. "Do you have any idea how many heifers I had to torture for the station manager to heed the murmurs of his men and call you people?" Genuine awe. "No matter. You, darling, passed my little test — and aren't you worth the wait! A challenge, at long last…"

*Backpackers? But there'd been no human victims… Heifers; so he'd broken the females… And 'a new Overlander' — Jesus, how many-*

Outwardly, Nancy laughed. "Speaking of Overlanders, you might want to get ready for a few of my mates."

"I think not. You're the only Overlander for a hundred kilometres."

She snorted. "Right, and you know this how?"

The vampire's lip twitched into a broad smile. "Oh, 'Tommo' and I had a little chat." He winked. "He says… Farewell."

*Shit…* Tom was Tima's Station Manager. And if he'd gotten to Tom… *Think!* Overlander protocol meant Tima would've only received

her name, her date of arrival — based on how far she had to travel —
and her quote. A grim blessing. Because if this one knew her
reputation… "And you're the only vampire here," she guessed.
"Now…"

He looked her right in the eye. "I am."

*Good.* Nancy shot him.

But in the split-second between her squeezing the trigger and
the chamber releasing her bullet, he dove for her legs, throwing her
backwards. As she fell, he flipped to his feet, his wounded leg landing
the jump. Her five minutes were up.

"Ironic," he purred, "that you're here posing as delicious bait,
and yet I managed to out-bait *you.*" He kicked the weapons from her
hands and poised his foot above her ribcage — her heart. And began to
press down. Nancy shoved and beat at him, his force the weight of a
supernatural slab. She could feel her bones straining to uphold, tissues
close to bursting. "There is no cavalry to come, my dear. So you may as
well admit defeat…" He smiled, dark and deadly, fangs indenting his
lower lip. "Unless you shall have violence."

Nancy swallowed a snarl. She'd *love* some violence, but she was
now at the disadvantage. Yet the game hadn't changed… Maybe she
could still be bait. She laboured beneath his boot. "Who are you?"

The vampire tilted his head. "I wouldn't get attached."

Nancy rolled her eyes, grimacing. "Yeah, well, I'm clearly not
going anywhere. What's wrong, afraid you'll bore me?" She grunted,
struggling some more.

"You may call me Victoire." His eyes narrowed. "For the time that you have left."

*Careful.* He could still snap her neck in half a heartbeat. "Victoire…" She let the name roll off her tongue, resting her palms on his dress shoes. "Look, I'm just here to do a job — which is clearly off. Can't we find some way to… Compromise?" She pouted, pressing her biceps together and accentuating the curves of her cleavage. God, she hated this shit… But she was out of options. He was silent. But his gaze descended to the desired spot.

*She would not kneel helpless.*

"I thought so," she said, her voice low and dark. Victoire's attention diverted, she struck the inside of his ankle, causing him to fall and catch himself atop her, swift as a panther. She let a lascivious grin flicker across her face, then wrapped her legs around him and squeezed with her thigh and calf muscles, bringing her heels within her grasp… Only to slide a gold hunting knife from her boot, and stab for his heart through his back.

He stilled, and she rolled him from her, climbing to her feet and pulling back to inspect her handiwork. Then choked on arid air. She was out, by mere millimetres — again. *Son of a bitch…* Nancy leapt back, too late. Victoire twisted, yanked her blade with effort and tossed it, then grabbed her by the throat as her boots left the ground, the casual vice of his deathly grasp forcing the breath from her windpipe.

*Overconfidence,* she thought absently. That had been her downfall.

"Pity," Victoire murmured, "though you're not the first to resort to feminine wiles." That sadistic smile. "And you won't be the last." He extended a vampiric claw, tracing a thin, bloody line from her chin all the way to the cleft between her breasts. Nancy thrashed, swinging both legs to kick off his chest, a move she'd performed too many times to count. But he was strong. At least the more oxygen she used, the faster she'd pass out; then she'd be unconscious for what came next. Because a woman Overlander, cut off and captured by a serial-killing vampire in the outback... She knew exactly what came next.

But Nancy's consciousness held, long enough for him to feed. His breath wintry on her neck, he plunged his fangs into her carotid — blood spewing from the puncture wounds. The coldness didn't dull the jagged agony, a pain she'd never contemplated, not once, in her near-decade of hunting the undead. She squeezed her eyes shut, but her life was draining fast, so fast... Groggily, she remembered the gold dust on her neck. But it wasn't working? Her eyes began to flutter closed, light fading, a sepia hue blotting and blurring her vision.

She was dying... And she couldn't stand the goddamn thought. The sorrow. The *fear*. She felt fifteen again, friends splayed, bloodied and broken, around the bonfire as she'd returned from the country show, big bag of marshmallows slipping from her fingers. She'd never screamed like that, before or since; like those girls in horror movies. A ghastly high-pitched wail that set her body quaking. And when the vampire — the very first vampire she'd ever met — had grabbed her, forced her to her grass-stained knees... She knew: this was it. And that mortal fear had *burned* inside her, at the thought of dying there, alone... Helpless.

Only she hadn't died that night. An Overlander had been casing the fair and heard her screams, and that Overlander — her mentor Rae, a fiery force of gold-forged will — had beheaded the vampire, saved her life and introduced her to the Overlanders. And set her on her current path... To never, ever kneel again.

But she'd lost her way. Too long since her last close call, too far removed from her beginnings — when fifteen-year-old Nancy had stared death in the face. She'd gotten cocky, traded years of fear for an arrogance that would eventually get her killed. It was a mistake. She saw that now. She saw... Everything.

She was alone. And she would die here. Her fear, the past, it all still burned... But she'd never kneeled. She was an Overlander... And it was always meant to end like this.

Nancy's grey eyes, flaring gold, shut on a haze of reddish-brown, followed by the colours of the... Rainbow? *Wait...* Not reddish-brown. *Terracotta, the colour of the land.* Real and raw and resplendent in its unbroken beauty.

And then... She felt it. Light, heat.

Victoire recoiled from her, eyes bulging. Scratching at his throat. Nancy collapsed to her knees. "Get it out..." He whispered. Her eyes couldn't, wouldn't focus. *Was he retching?*

"Get it out." He snarled, claws drawing his own blood now, mad slashes and gashes. "GET IT OUT!" He gurgled a scream, to someone, not her, not her... She tried and failed to get onto her elbows, gulping air. And then he too was falling, convulsing on the ground, heart hammering metal. She saw him rise, begging for mercy. "Out…" That colour, terracotta. So familiar… Dipping, shaking, dancing…

Nancy's eyes flew open. *The magic of the bush.*

A low whistle, the unmistakable sound of a spear — the first hunters' weapon — thrown true… And a seven-foot shaft was sticking from Victoire's chest.

This one hadn't missed.

Nancy's head lolled to the side. Victoire was dead on the dirt and decomposing fast. *Pretty*, she thought, staring at the terracotta pattern on the spear's handle. Her eyes, gold fading to grey, rolled back in her head as she yielded to unconsciousness. But before she did, she sensed a figure crouched beside her… Dark hands pressed to her bleeding neck… Then light. Heat. She knew the tribal name of the people living on Country around here, but she couldn't remember, couldn't remember…

A voice. Gentle. Kind. "Never helpless." Then, words she didn't understand. No. Couldn't remember… A hand on her head. "You're safe here. Sleep."

Finally… Darkness.

Nancy awoke to the sky raining *plish plosh* droplets on her face. *Rain…?* She sat up and winced, expecting her head to pound. It didn't. She froze, then sprang to her feet as she began to remember. Her hand flew to her neck — but there were no wounds. She whirled to where she'd last seen the vampire, Victoire. Nothing but the gilded shadows of an outback sunrise, terracotta dirt shimmering in the rain. She looked down and saw a blade of grass poking from beneath her boot. Hope, rain, life… In the middle of the Australian desert.

She remembered something else, but it felt like a dream. Words someone had told her. When? She didn't know… She only knew what they meant.

*Poison of the Rainbow Serpent.*

Nancy spun in a slow circle as a new day dawned. When she was finally convinced she was alone, the Overlander returned to Tima Cattle Station.

Humble… Human. And never helpless. Because she knew how Victoire had died.

Magic — and her blood, now weaponised with liquid sun-fire gold.

Nancy's blood could now kill a vampire.


**Amy de la Force** is an Australian fantasy and supernatural writer, ex-Apple creative, and queen of random hobbies (think kung fu and sword fighting). She's also a member of the Australian Society of Authors. Amy lives in London with her husband and cheeky child. Tweet her at @amydelaforce.

# Thank you…

Readers are why we do what we do to bring these stories to the world. We hope you enjoyed this collection as much as we enjoyed reading all the submissions ourselves. We'd love it if you would let us know what you think by leaving a review on Amazon, Goodreads, or wherever you can. You may want to try some of our other collections. A full list is available on our website:

https://www.cloakedpress.com

Happy Reading from the Cloaked Press Family.

Manufactured by Amazon.ca
Bolton, ON

15247523R00143